# BLOOD BOUND

IDELLA BREEN

This is a work of fiction. Any businesses, locations, and organizations mentioned, while real, are used in a way that is purely fictional.

First Printing, 2016

www.idellabreen.com

Formatted with Vellum

# ALSO BY IDELLA BREEN

The Dance of The Firefly

When The Clock Strikes Nothing

Fire& Ice:

Blood Bound

Soul Awakened

Lover Eternal/Adventures of Elena the Werewolf

Pack Mentality

The King of Brimstone and Bones

Blood & Ember:

Blood Eternal: Book One of Salt

Witch Twin Chronicles:

Unrestricted Magic

Eternal Soul Trilogy:

Bone Walker

Water & Bone:

The Girl Who Leapt Worlds

Novellas:

Feeders and Bleeders

Descent

*For Hazel, thank you for keeping my love of reading alive.*

# CHAPTER ONE

Cait Fallon, Ms. Fallon to her students, paused before opening the door to her classroom and turned to the transfer student behind her. The girl's name was Snow Bennett, and like most of the students in her grade, she had just turned eighteen. Cait couldn't help but stare at the girl. She had grown so much. The redhead could remember seeing Snow when she was still in diapers, but even though she knew of Snow, the brunette didn't know of her. Cait hadn't seen her since she was just a baby, and she had made Snow's mother, Integra, promise never to tell her daughter of the promise Cait had made to Lidia, Snow's grandmother.

"Are you ready?" Cait asked.

Snow took a deep breath before nodding. Cait smiled, then opened the door. The scene they walked into was one unique to their type of school. The room was in absolute chaos. One kid, a tengu, or crow demon, was flying around the classroom while another boy with an extremely long neck, a rokurokubi, was trying to catch him between his jaws. A girl was singing an alluring tune to another boy. He looked dazed, while she looked as if she was about to take a bite out of him. Cait sighed before taking command. She turned back to Snow.

"Wait here. I'll formally introduce you."

The brunette nodded. Cait turned back to her new students for the year. She clapped her hands, getting their attention. "Takeshi, come down from the ceiling and take your seat. Jared, pull your neck back in before I chop it off and Sarah, quit singing before the whole class falls asleep."

Within minutes, all the students were in their seats and facing forward. Cait smiled. It seemed her reputation preceded her. Guess it helped when most of the school feared her losing her temper. She nodded; as they should. Cait walked to the front of the room where the chalkboard and lectern were. She set down her seating chart, looked up at the students she would be teaching for the year, and smiled. Another mixed bunch. She looked forward to whipping them into shape. Even though this was a monster high school, it was still her job to get the students ready to face the outside world.

"Good morning, everyone."

"Good morning, Ms. Fallon," they replied in unison. Cait smiled. Whatever rumor the previous seniors had passed along was working wonders.

"We have a new transfer student today. I know it's only the second day of school, but I want you all to give her a warm welcome and help her get settled in. Come on in, Snow."

Cait had to hand it to her. The girl walked in with an air of authority and confidence, and stood by her facing the class.

"This is Snow Bennett. She will be in our class this year. You can take your seat next to Sarah. Sarah, can you raise your hand please?" Snow smiled back at Cait and whispered a quick thank you before walking towards her seat. Cait felt her stomach flutter and swallowed. Maybe she was nervous to be teaching another class this year. She turned back to her class.

"I'm going to lay down a few ground rules for this homeroom. First of all, I don't mind if you do your homework here so long as you stand during the pledge, and at least half listen to morning announcements. What I will not tolerate are any shenanigans or foul play. You will behave yourselves in this classroom or you'll piss me off, and I'll tell you right now, you really don't want to see me mad." She saw the students take a collective gulp.

"Now, that being said, I understand you have certain needs depending on what you are. Don't be afraid to ask for help. I might look young, but I know a lot more than you do. Any questions?"

One student raised his hand. Cait looked down at her seating chart. "Yes, Cole?"

"How old are you?"

Cait smiled. "How old do you think I am?"

All the students stilled and seemed to be holding their breath.

"Um, twenty?"

She nodded. "Works for me. Now, let me turn on morning announcements." With that, she picked up the remote from the lectern, switched on the television in the corner of the classroom, then took her seat at her desk in the back of the room. The whole room seemed to let out a collective breath as each student went about their own business, some pulling out homework they didn't finish the night before, while others whispered quietly among themselves. Cait couldn't help but look up and search for Snow.

The girl was whispering to Sarah, and the two seemed to be getting along. Cait smiled and started pulling out her work. She felt like she always had something to do these days. Being a teacher in the modern day was a hell of a lot more work than it used to be.

SNOW WAS MYSTIFIED and intrigued by her homeroom teacher, Ms. Fallon. The woman didn't look a day over twenty, but she held herself with such confidence that it commanded the attention of everyone in the room. She seemed like a nice woman, though. When Ms. Fallon had spoken to her earlier, it was done in a familiar way, almost as if she knew her. Snow was sure she had never met her homeroom teacher before today. The woman really was a mystery. Her mane of long, red hair was kept in a high ponytail, and she was slender, but not skinny. She was really tall, too. Much taller than the brunette's five-foot-eight-inches in height. Ms. Fallon moved in a graceful way, unlike Snow's own clumsy bumbles. It was almost predatorily. Snow began to wonder what exactly Ms. Fallon was while she sat down next to Sarah.

"Hello, my name is Sarah Ginn, and I'm a siren." Sarah held out her hand as she boasted. Snow was shocked for a moment, as she had never met another person that immediately said what exactly they were. It was usually an unspoken agreement that most people would try to keep that information to themselves for fear of showing their weakness. She was hesitant to return the favor, so instead, she simply shook the girl's hand. "I'm Snow. It's nice to meet you."

"So why did you transfer here? Did you just move here with your parents?"

She had been anticipating this question, but now that it was asked, she was hesitant to answer. "Actually, I just moved here by myself."

"You're living by yourself?"

"Yeah. My eighteenth birthday was last week."

"Wow. Why are you even going to school then? I would like, totally drop out if I was eighteen."

"I just want to finish. My mom went to this school. It's where she met my dad. I just kind of want to see it for myself, you know?"

"That's so romantic!"

Snow smiled, but was startled by the bell ringing.

"What's your first class?"

Snow pulled out her schedule. "I have English first."

"Ah, I have Calculus. Who's your teacher?"

Snow glanced behind her to the woman working at the desk in the back of the classroom. She turned back to Sarah. "Ms. Fallon."

Sarah nodded. "Well, I hear she's a really good teacher despite the not so subtle threats she gave out this morning. Just don't piss her off and your day will go smoothly."

Snow smiled as her seat buddy packed her bag and left the room along with the mob of students. Looking around, she realized there were only two other students in the classroom. One was the tengu boy, the one that had been flying around the classroom earlier. The other was a boy on the other side of the classroom sitting in the back. He was bent over his desk scribbling away on a piece of paper. Suddenly, he looked up and met her gaze. She sucked in a sharp breath. His eyes were two glowing red orbs staring back at her. She was used to seeing red eyes. Her grandmother had them as well, though hers had been much kinder. This boy's scared her. He was a vampire, and he looked hungry.

Snow's gaze was broken as other students filed into the room taking their seats, and she turned to face the front. Taking several deep breaths, she tried to get her heart to settle. Whoever that boy was, she was going to stay the hell away from him. Her thoughts were interrupted by the earthy smell of fresh rain. She immediately felt herself relax.

"Are you okay, Snow?"

She looked up. It was Ms. Fallon.

Snow nodded.

"If you need anything, don't hesitate to ask. I promise I don't bite." The redhead smiled.

Snow giggled. She couldn't help the calming effect that Ms. Fallon seemed to have on her. It was like she just knew that if anyone messed with her, Ms. Fallon would step in and always be on her side. She shook the feeling off as she watched her teacher walk to the front of the room and begin her lecture.

"Okay, class, today we will be starting one of the books off your reading list. I hope you all brought Frankenstein, Jezera's edition."

"Wait, we weren't supposed to get Mary Shelley's Frankenstein?" one kid yelled out.

Cait sighed and thought, We get one every year. "Don't worry, I have a few spares."

"What's the difference?" the same kid asked.

"There is a huge difference. Mary Shelley's is the classic, but Jezera's edition is more of a meditation on the actual life of Frankenstein and how he took on the name of his creator and survived until this modern day."

"You mean Frankenstein is alive?"

"Don't you know?" another kid snickered.

"Enough of that. To answer your question, yes, Frankenstein is still alive. He lives in Alaska with his family. Jezera interviewed him several years ago, and this book is the result of that interview," Cait said.

"What's it about?"

"Well, you'll just have to read it and find out, now won't you." Cait placed a spare copy of the book down on the boy's desk and turned around to retreat to her own desk. "Go ahead and read for the rest of this class. I don't want to see anyone working on other homework."

Snow waited until Ms. Fallon took her seat before walking over to her desk. Cait looked up from the paperwork she was filling out. "Yes, Snow?"

Snow felt her stomach flutter at the way her name sounded coming from the redhead. It always came out as a song. "Ms. Fallon, I don't have the book. I lost it while moving here."

Cait nodded and picked up one of the spares from the corner of her desk and handed it to the brunette. When their hands met briefly, it felt like an electric shock traveled up Snow's arm and settled in her chest. Snow jerked her hand back and the book fell to the desk.

"Sorry!" she rushed out.

Cait stared at her hand in shock before shaking her head, handing the book back to Snow, careful not to make skin contact. "It's fine. It was probably just static. You can borrow the book if you like. Until you get your own."

"Are you sure that's okay?"

"Yeah, they're mine. I don't mind sharing." Cait smiled, and Snow smiled back as butterflies were released in her stomach again. What was that?

"Thank you."

"You'd better get to reading."

Snow nodded and went back to her desk. Cait watched before turning back to the forms she was filling out. What had that electric shock been? It had gone straight up her hand and to her heart in seconds. She could still feel the residual tingles of it. She needed to speak with the principal about this. He knew a lot more about her species than she did. She had no one else really to turn to, after all. Cait felt the familiar anger bubble up in her gut, blocking out the earlier pleasurable feeling, but she squashed it back down and refocused on the forms in front of her. She would speak with the principal when school was over. It was never good when something new popped up with her, whether it was a new feeling or whatever. It usually meant something bad; or so experience had taught her.

# CHAPTER TWO

The end of the day couldn't come fast enough Cait thought as she marched down the empty hallways towards the principal's office. She had been feeling off ever since the morning, and she didn't know why. Well, she knew why. It had to do with that electric shock she had felt come out of Snow. It had thrown her out of whack or something. She had been short with her students, putting them on their best behavior so as not to get her any more riled up than she already was.

The rumor going around was that a student had forgotten his book in the morning class and asked a bunch of dumb questions that pissed her off. Cait snorted. Like that would piss her off for a whole day. She had more control over herself than that—or so she thought. The tingles from the morning were still running throughout her body, making her other half bump up against her mental cage. It was really making her antsy and irritable.

She needed to speak with Remus. He knew more about this stuff than she did. He still had his clan to teach him these things. When she reached his office, she didn't bother with knocking and burst through the door, only to pause mid-step.

Snow was sitting in one of the chairs across from Remus holding an ice pack up to the side of her face. Cait took a whiff and caught the scent of fresh blood coming from the girl. Her other half rammed up against her mental cage. Through sheer willpower, she physically restrained herself by gripping the doorjamb, holding herself in place. That didn't stop the snarl coming out of her as she turned to Remus.

"What the hell happened?"

Remus gave her a leveled look, calculating. "Cait, I'm busy at the moment. Can you come back later?"

"I asked what happened?" Like hell she was coming back later. Snow was hers to protect. She had promised. A blood pact.

Remus looked from her face to her death grip on his door. "I'm trying to figure that out right now. If you could—"

Snow whimpered as she moved the ice to a tender spot. Cait barged into the room and shut the door behind her. She immediately squatted next to Snow to be at her level.

"Are you okay, Snow?"

Snow nodded.

"Can I look at it?"

The girl removed the ice pack to show the damage. A large gash ran from her temple to the middle of her cheek. There was a salve on it, and it had been stitched up well. The nurse's station at Monster High was basically a hospital due to the dangerous nature of the children that attended the school. Cait let out a breath between her teeth and gently tilted Snow's chin so she could get a better look.

"What happened, Snow?" Cait asked softly.

Snow felt herself relax under Cait's gaze. She felt her mouth moving of its own volition. "I got into a fight in the girl's bathroom, with a harpy."

"What? Why?"

"She said I didn't smell right. That I smelt like a half-blood. What's a half-blood?"

Cait pulled back her hand as she felt her claws beginning to come out. She didn't want to hurt Snow. "It's nothing. I mean, it's not a bad thing."

Cait was struggling to keep her voice level. She didn't want to scare the girl next to her, but her other half was biting and scratching at her mental cage. It was demanding the blood of the harpy. "What was her name? Who was she?"

Snow opened her mouth as if to answer but Remus interrupted, "Snow, you can leave now. We will continue this tomorrow after school. I need to speak with Ms. Fallon right now."

The brunette nodded but didn't move from her seat. She didn't want to leave Cait's presence just to go home to an empty house filled with boxes she still had to unpack. It was weird. She didn't know why, but she suddenly didn't want to go home at all, when only minutes ago she had been trying to find an excuse to leave the principal's office without telling him what happened.

Remus cleared his throat, getting both Snow and Cait's attention. He stood and walked around his desk, helping Snow stand up.

"Mary? Come here please," Remus called out. The door to his office opened and a woman with striking green eyes and a leopard's tail came into the room. "Yes, Remus?"

"Can you please take Ms. Bennett home. She is injured, and the buses have already left."

"Of course." Mary made to move forward but was intercepted by Cait, who glared at her. Mary looked unsure and turned to Remus. He sighed. He would have to do this carefully. He had no command over Cait, and she seemed to be quickly losing control. He would have to plead with her other half. Remus leaned down to whisper in Snow's ear.

"I need you to say that you are okay and that you want Mary to take you home."

Snow looked up at him, startled. "But—"

"I really need you to say it, Snow. I need your help with this one."

"But I—"

"You will see Ms. Fallon tomorrow, I promise. You have her as your homeroom teacher, right?"

Snow nodded.

"Don't you want to go home and rest? I'm sure you're tired."

She nodded again.

"Good, so can you please say what I asked you to?"

Snow looked unsure, as if she was fighting her own inner battle. Remus could smell her confusion. She seemed to win this time and turned to look to where Cait was glaring down Mary.

"I'm okay, Ms. Fallon. I want Mary to take me home."

Cait's head jerked in her direction and she had a kicked puppy look on her face. Snow almost changed her mind, but Remus gripped her shoulder to remind her.

"Really, I'm okay. I just want to go home, and I want Mary to take me."

Cait seemed to be struggling to find her words. She nodded and moved aside while looking down at the floor. Mary quickly moved and swept Snow away before the girl had a chance to change her mind.

"I'll see you tomorrow, Ms. Fallon," Snow whispered as she walked by.

The room was still after the two left. Remus moved back around his desk to take a seat. "Please, sit."

Cait's movements were jerky as she maneuvered herself into the chair Snow had occupied only moments before.

"I take it you have some questions?" Remus's voice was level and soothing. As if to placate.

Cait nodded. She couldn't think straight. She should be the one taking Snow home, not that other woman. She was Snow's teacher. Why did Snow say she wanted Mary to take her home? Was she really going to be okay?

Her thoughts were interrupted by Remus's calm voice. "Cait?"

She met his gaze. "Remus, what's happening to me?"

He nodded. This was the problem when a person didn't have their clan to teach them. Cait had been so young when her clan was massacred. He sighed. "Did you make any physical contact with Snow earlier today? Like, was there any type of, I guess some would call it a static shock, or warmth?"

Cait nodded. "It was earlier today. Our hands met, and I felt an electric shock from it. It felt like it traveled straight to my heart. What's wrong with me, Remus?"

"It's for reasons like this that I wish you had accepted my offer to join my pack, Cait. This could be very dangerous for both you and Snow. You're a lone wolf with no master, no alpha."

"What's so dangerous? What are you talking about?"

Remus sighed. "What do you know about imprinting?"

"Not a lot. Just that it's how my parents met. They said it was when you fall in love with someone."

Remus laughed. "You must have been very young when

you asked. Imprinting is when a werewolf meets their soul mate. Their one true mate. They bond with that person for eternity."

"What exactly are you saying, Remus?"

"That feeling you felt when you touched Snow. That's what it feels like to touch your imprint. It's how you know you've met your soulmate. Usually, I'd say congratulations, but like I was saying earlier, this could be dangerous for the both of you. When a wolf first finds their imprint, a few things have to occur before the human side can regain control of the wolf."

"I imprinted?"

"Yes, Cait. You imprinted. On Snow."

"How is that even possible?"

He smiled. "Why wouldn't it be? Did you never think you would find your imprint?"

"Not in this lifetime. Not after what I've done."

His smile fell. "But you did. Now, there are some choices you need to make."

"Why is it dangerous?"

"As I was saying, a few things need to occur so you can stay in control. Usually, the alpha of the pack would take control over your wolf until you have finally completed the blood bond. Only then would you have the strength to take back control over your wolf."

"But I don't have an alpha."

"Therein lies the danger. Snow is a half-blood—"

Cait growled, "Don't call her that!"

"I'm sorry, but it's the truth. Her father was human and her mother a salamander. She is essentially human but with an ability passed down from her bloodline. I understand her grandmother had the same ability?"

Cait nodded. "She did."

"Werewolves rarely mate to humans in this day and age. They usually imprint on stronger races. It's in our DNA to seek out strong mates. The ones that do mate to humans usually have an alpha to help with the mating ceremony."

"I refuse to bow my head to you, Remus. You are a good friend, but I'm also an alpha. I won't bow to another."

Remus sighed. "You always did come from a proud people. The Fallons were a great clan. May they rest in peace."

"What would happen in the case when an alpha imprinted?"

"The omega would take on his wolf."

"The omega?"

"What do you remember of your omega?"

"She wasn't a strong woman, but everyone in the pack respected her. She was definitely smaller than our alpha, my father, though. How could she handle an alpha's wolf?"

"The alpha of a clan protects their omega. A clan that can keep their omega alive is a proud and strong one. An alpha would never attack their omega, the weakest wolf of the pack. The omegas have a calming effect on the whole clan. Most werewolf packs are volatile, but their omega helps the clan stay together by calming the younger wolves, as well as the more short-tempered ones."

"What about their mate?"

"The mate can only do so much until the blood bond is complete; only then will they be able to handle their mate's wolf. Wolves are territorial. What would you have done to that harpy?"

Cait growled. "I'd rip her wings off and feed them to her!"

Remus chuckled. "Exactly. Would you have normally reacted that way if it was another student?"

She sighed and said, "I see your point, Remus, but I refuse to join your pack."

"Pride can be a dangerous thing, Cait."

"I'm a bad luck charm for any clan, Remus."

"That's silly."

The redhead stood. "Say what you will, but I know what I know. I'm going home. I need to think."

He sighed. "I advise you to think quickly. I've never seen a bond form quite so strongly, or quickly, between both the wolf and the mate. You two may both need the guidance I can offer."

"I'll think on it. Goodbye."

Cait closed the office door and made her way past Mary's desk. She glared at it but shook her head to clear her mind. This was bad. Remus was right. How was she going to handle this if it was so strong? This need to claim what was hers. Next thing she knew, she'd be peeing on Snow to mark her territory. Cait shuddered at the thought.

# CHAPTER THREE

Mary pulled into Snow's apartment building's parking lot and cut the engine.

"Would you like me to walk you up to your apartment?"

When the girl didn't immediately answer, Mary looked over to see that she was staring out the window, as if in a daze.

"Snow?"

The brunette jerked, startled, and turned to the leopard. "Yes?"

"We're here. Come on; I'll walk you to your apartment."

"Okay." Snow unbuckled her seat belt and climbed out of the tan Honda Civic. The leopard met her on the other side of the car, her tail flicking languidly behind her.

"Shall we go?" Mary asked. Snow nodded and followed her.

"Ms. Mary?"

"I don't mind if you just call me Mary." She smiled, her green eyes lighting with humor.

"Mary, then. Forgive me if I'm overstepping my bounds, but are you a werecat?"

Mary continued to smile. "It's no problem. I am, and I'm proud to be one. It's kind of hard for me to hide it, after all." Her tail flicked lazily, bringing a smile to Snow's face.

"Why do you ask?"

"You reminded me of someone I knew. She used to be my bodyguard before I left home but I never had the courage to ask what she was. Probably because she's been watching me ever since I was little. She doesn't have a tail like you, though."

"Mmm, I'm still young in werecat terms. I'm a little under a hundred. So, I'm still learning to hide my nature. Why do you think we are alike?"

"She moves with the same grace as you and has similar eyes. They are more hazel, though."

"I see. Well, I don't know her, but I would have to agree with your judgment. Why were you afraid to ask her what she was?"

"She's kind of unapproachable. Very stoic, but still kind."

"I see. Well, it seems her job was to protect you, so I can understand her need for distance."

They climbed onto the elevator and Snow pressed the button for the fourth floor. "Do you know Ms. Fallon well?"

Mary's tail paused a moment before picking up its lazy swishing. "Not particularly. I know Remus better, and he knows her well."

"Oh, okay."

"Why do you ask?"

Snow shrugged. "I was just wondering."

Mary smiled. The elevator doors opened and Mary

followed the girl's lead down the hallway. "Do you know her well?"

Snow stopped mid-step before resuming to her door. She pulled out her keys. "I don't know. I don't think so." She paused and stared at the door to her apartment. Apartment 401.

"You don't think?" Mary urged.

Snow sighed. "I don't know; I just feel like I know her from somewhere. Like from when I was really little, but I just can't seem to remember."

"Oh."

Snow turned to look at the leopard. "Is that strange?"

Mary shook her head. "I don't think so. I've learned in my lifetime to trust my gut, or in my case, my instinct."

"But, she didn't act like she knew me from anywhere."

Mary nodded. "Maybe she doesn't want you to know that she knows you."

"What do you mean?"

"Oh, nothing."

"What do you know, Mary?"

"What don't I know?"

Snow laughed. "Is getting a leopard to give a straight answer always so hard?"

"Is it?"

"Fine, okay. I'll figure it out myself. You're worse than my bodyguard," Snow sniggered.

Snow unlocked the front door and walked through the entrance before turning back to Mary. "Thank you for driving me home."

"It's no problem..." She trailed off as she caught a glimpse of all the boxes inside the apartment. "Did you just move in?"

Snow glanced behind and blushed. "Kind of."

Mary chuckled. "I'm going to go out on a limb. Would you like me to help you unpack? I don't know if you know many people around here, and no offense, but you don't look very muscular."

"Um, you have no idea how happy I would be if you helped me. I really don't have any friends here, and I was dreading having to unpack all of these boxes by myself."

"It would be my pleasure. My schedule was clear for the rest of the day anyway." Mary smiled and walked past Snow, pouncing on the first box in front of her. "Let's get to work!" she sang.

A GROWL RIPPED from Cait's throat as her fist flew out, connecting with the purple padded helmet of her opponent. The man's head snapped back and he dropped like a fly. Cait pulled her mouth guard out, panting as she walked to her corner and grabbed a towel. Nathan was waiting for her with a lopsided grin on his face. The jagged purple stripes on each side of his face moved as he spoke and ran a hand through his military-cut white hair.

"Think you're done beating up my students today? I don't think any more of them will be willing to get in the ring with you, even if I paid them," he chuckled.

Cait grunted, took the towel that he offered to wipe the sweat from her brow, and took a drink from her water bottle.

"Come on; I deserve more than a grunt. What's up today? The last time you took out ten of my top students in a row was when your last girlfriend cheated on you with that succubus."

"I never liked that bitch."

"That's beside the point. What's eating at you?" Nathan followed her as she climbed out of the ring and sat down on a bench. The students that had gathered around scattered like ants and refused to make eye contact, as if she would gobble them up.

"You wouldn't understand."

"Give me a little credit. I may be younger than you, but I've seen a lot in my time, being what I am."

"I don't know, Nathan. I don't really want to talk about it. It makes me mad just thinking about it."

"Come on! Talking about stuff is the way it gets better."

The redhead sighed. She could use another perspective, and Nathan knew how to keep a secret. "Just don't tell anyone. It's kind of personal."

Nathan sat down next to her and looked up at his students, who were a little too close for Cait's comfort. "All right, everyone, hit the showers. I don't want to see you smelly gorillas until tomorrow."

The students scattered again, but this time towards the locker room. They couldn't get away fast enough. "You should come here more often. It helps keep their egos in check," he laughed.

Cait sighed again.

"So what's the problem? Girl trouble again? Need me to beat anyone up for you?"

The werewolf cracked a smile at that. Nathan had always been like a big brother to her. He was always there to make her laugh or just hear out her problems whenever she needed someone to lend their ear.

"I've imprinted."

His smile dropped. "Shit."

Cait frowned. "You know what that means?"

"What? You didn't?"

"No, actually. Remus just told me today, after it happened."

"Didn't your clan ever teach you about it?"

Cait's features darkened and she simply said, "No."

He studied her curiously. "Huh, usually that's taught to a pup when they hit puberty."

"How do you know what it is?"

"Haven't you figured out what I am yet?" he chuckled, trying to lighten the mood.

She stared at him thoughtfully for a moment. "No."

"I guess I'll just tell you then. It was a fun game while it lasted, but you won't understand how I know about imprinting until I tell you."

"Okay."

"Drum roll please!"

Cait chuckled.

"I'm an inuyoukai."

"A dog demon?"

"Our species are very similar. We don't imprint, but we do have one true mate. I just know what imprinting is from what my mentors in my pack told me. We are taught our similarities to other species as well as our differences."

"I've heard of inuyoukai, but I had never met one. Or at least, I didn't think I had. How come you don't smell like a dog?"

Nathan grinned. "What do I smell like?"

"Spicy. Hot. Most dogs that I meet, or at least shapeshifters that shift into dogs, smell earthy. Even most werewolves smell earthy."

"That's the demon in me you're smelling. Or at least that's the best explanation I can come up with. It's how I always describe it to other shifters or werebeasts."

"Oh, that makes sense then."

Nathan clapped his hands. "So you met your imprint? Is she everything you imagined and more? Most people are happy to meet their soulmate. Why are you so pissed?"

"I'm not really mad..." she trailed off as Nathan gave her a look that said, tell that to my students. "Okay, but it's mostly my wolf that is mad. It wants to be with my imprint. Like right now. But I can't be."

"Why not? Isn't it bad to be away from them? Especially in the beginning?"

"Why in the beginning?"

Nathan shrugged. "I don't know how much werebeasts, werewolves in particular, share in common with our demon customs, but in the beginning, when an inuyoukai meets their mate, there is an overwhelming need to stake their claim so no one else will try and claim them. The only way I can describe it is, primal."

Cait studied him. "I do feel a strong tug on my instincts to be near, and to mark my territory, but Remus said it would be dangerous without another alpha or omega present."

Nathan nodded. "Remus is that werewolf friend that is also your boss?"

She nodded.

"Well, he would know more than I would. But isn't he also the guy that keeps trying to claim you in his clan?"

She nodded again.

"I would take what he says with a grain of salt. I don't fully know your situation, but he might use all of this against you. Isn't there someone in your own clan that can help you? I know you're not on the best terms with them, but you might need some counsel without ulterior motives."

Cait's features darkened again. "No. There is no one."

"Now isn't the time to be prideful or picky, Cait. There's a reason werewolves stay in their clan. I've never really commented on your whole lone wolf act. I've never understood it myself, but I've respected it. I really think now is the time to seek the counsel of your elders. I know you're an alpha, from your scent, but even an alpha needs to know when to ask for help."

Cait had stood during his lecture and began walking toward the locker rooms.

"Cait, are you listening to me?"

She stopped and turned on him when he reached for her shoulder. She snarled, and he held up his hands in surrender. Her eyes were hard when she spoke her next words and her voice sent a shiver of fear down Nathan's spine.

"They are all dead, Nathan. All of them. My whole clan. And I don't need you reminding me because of your ignorance. I have no one, and I don't need anyone. So, you can shove your lecture up your ass, or I'll do it for you." She turned on her heel and went straight to the front door. Screw getting her gym bag. She needed some air; just needed to get away from all these people with opinions on what she should do with her imprint. She needed to go for a drive. Cait slammed the door on her way out and didn't look back.

## CHAPTER
# FOUR

"You have no idea how grateful I am that you stayed," Snow said as she sat heavily on her clean couch. All the empty boxes had been thrown down the trash chute and everything was put in its proper place.

"It was my pleasure. I couldn't leave a weakling like you to try and do all the work by yourself. You probably would have hurt yourself."

"You damn werebeast. You have way too much strength and energy than you know what to do with. I wish you would share it with the rest of us." She laughed and threw an arm over her eyes as she lay her head back.

Mary looked down at her watch and sighed. "Well, it's getting late, and I need to make some dinner before I starve. All this strength and energy that seems endless to you is actually fueled with mountains of food and my tank is almost on empty."

Snow nodded and stood, but was interrupted by a yawn. "I'll walk you—to the door," she finished.

Mary chuckled. "It's okay. I can see myself out. Make

sure you find the energy to do your homework. And try not to oversleep and miss the bus."

"Thank you, Mary. I don't know what I would have done without your help."

Mary smiled and waved as she made her way down the hall to the front door. The brunette waited as she heard the door open but was surprised to hear another voice instead of the sound of the door closing.

"What are you doing here?" the female voice all but growled.

"I'm—"

"Get out of here!"

Snow jumped up quickly and ran down the hall. The other person at the door sounded ready to commit murder. She went around the corner and was surprised to see Ms. Fallon glaring at Mary. The poor leopard looked ready to pee her pants.

"Cait, it's not what you think. I would never take what's y—"

"I said get out!"

Snow felt the bite of hot anger burn her gut. How dare she speak to Mary like that after the leopard had been kind enough to help her unpack. Snow marched right past Mary and poked Cait in the chest with enough force to bruise a normal human, but Cait barely budged.

"How dare you speak to her like that in my house!" Snow yelled, trying to push the redhead back; but the woman seemed to be made of stone. Snow could see her muscles ripple through her shirt as they flexed, as if to hold back a movement. Cait stilled as she focused her electric-blue eyes on Snow.

Mary felt it was time to leave and slid past the two who had left just a big enough gap for the leopard to get past.

She slunk away down the hall without making a peep. She needed to call Remus. The leopard knew she wasn't strong enough to deal with an alpha. Especially one as old and battle-worn as Cait. Mary feared what might happen to Snow. She had really become attached to the girl in the short time they had together.

Cait stood in the doorway, coiled and taut, watching Snow while trying to rein in her other half. The wolf had nearly broken through her mental barrier and ripped Mary to shreds. How dare that woman go after what was hers! How dare she leave her scent all over her imprint and her apartment! This was hers. Mine!

"Are you listening to me, Ms. Fallon? You need to learn your place. This is my home! If Mary wants to be here, then she has my permission, and every right to be."

That caught her attention. "No, she doesn't!" Cait growled.

The brunette was stunned by the growl in her teacher's voice and stepped back. "What?"

Cait advanced as her alpha persona kicked in. Her mate needed to learn her place. "I said no, she doesn't."

Snow's cheeks puffed out as she poked her finger into the werewolf's chest again. "I said, she does."

"Do you choose her over me?" Cait breathed through her nose as she bit the inside of her cheek. She needed to gain control again. Her wolf was winning. She could feel her primal side taking over and the need to claim what was rightfully hers was growing stronger with every word. She needed to make her mate see that she was strong enough for her. Even if she had to do it forcefully.

Snow paused as what her teacher said registered in her hazy mind. "What?"

Cait moved forward as if she was stalking her prey and

gently grabbed Snow's finger, removing it from her chest and bringing it to her mouth, where she kissed it. "I asked if you chose her over me. I'm stronger, faster, and just better than her. Do you need me to prove it?" Slowly her tongue snaked out to wrap around Snow's finger, pulling it into the hot depths and sucking languidly on it. Snow felt the warmth travel from her hand straight down to her groin. Her cheeks flushed as she took another step back while trying to reclaim her hand. Cait moved with her. Her tongue was stroking the finger still in her mouth. Snow's legs suddenly felt like Jell-O; her hand shot out to the wall, helping her regain her balance. What was happening? Her whole body tingled as those electric-blue eyes bore into her.

"Ms. Fal—" Cait gently bit her finger before allowing it to slide slowly out of her mouth.

"Cait."

Snow was dazed as warmth surrounded her and Cait moved closer, caging the girl in between her arms and the wall. The werewolf kicked the door closed pulling Snow out into the hallway and nuzzled into Snow's neck, giving a testing lick.

"What?"

"I said, my name is Cait. Not Ms. Fallon."

Snow was quickly losing her train of thought as the woman in front of her began to lightly nibble on her neck. She just felt so hot. It was like Cait was a furnace, but it felt good. She wanted to be closer to that warmth. She had always been so cold due to her ability. The warmth of the woman in front of her was intoxicating. In the back of her mind, she felt like something was wrong. There was danger, but she didn't know where, and her mind was too hazy to remember what they had been talking about. She whispered out, "Cait."

"Yes, that's right," Cait breathed as her hand teased the bottom of Snow's school polo. One hand was resting on Snow's waist while the other dared to slip under the polo to meet the warm skin of the girl's stomach. They both gasped at the contact and the shock that traveled between them.

"Cait!" Snow gasped and leaned fully back into the wall as the woman settled against her body.

"I'll make you forget that leopard."

Leopard. Who was that again? Snow thought as something hot and wet dipped into her ear before pulling out, only to be replaced by teeth that gently nibbled on the outer shell. Hot breath fanned against her cheek as soft lips brushed their way back down her neck and to her collarbone.

"Wait. I think...I think we should stop."

Cait didn't even pause. "Why?"

"I'm not sure..." Snow trailed off as the hand that had been rubbing circles around her bellybutton suddenly traveled higher to tickle just underneath her bra.

"You're mine, Snow. I don't share well." Cait bit Snow's collarbone, making the girl gasp before she soothed it with her tongue.

"Yours?" Snow mumbled.

Cait nodded as her hand finally slipped under her bra and made contact. Snow gasped and gripped at Cait's arm.

"Wait."

"No. I want you. Now." She circled the girl's nipple, making it harden before she pinched.

Snow to cried out, "Cait! Don't..."

Cait ducked her head down and her mouth replaced her

hand. Snow's head slammed against the wall as her nipple was sucked and nibbled on. She could feel herself getting wet between her legs and rubbed them together, hoping to get some friction. She was so hot. Cait's other hand traveled down and coerced the brunette's legs open. The werewolf quickly settled between them and gasped out as wet met hard abs.

"Snow, you're killing me," the werewolf groaned.

The girl had begun to rub herself against Cait, trying to get more friction as she moaned out. "Don't stop."

Cait gripped her ass, pulling her harder against her as Snow wrapped her legs around the redhead's waist. One hand supported the girl as the werewolf licked and sucked on a breast. She pulled the nipple into her mouth and twirled her tongue around it, eliciting another moan.

"Please..." Snow trailed off.

"Say you're mine," Cait growled.

"I'm not..."

"Say it." Cait bit her nipple and Snow cried out as she rubbed herself harder against hard abs.

"I'm—"

Whatever Snow was going to say was cut off, leaving only coldness. A snarl filled the air, and it took a minute for Snow to register what had happened. She stumbled back into the wall, as Cait had been holding her but had suddenly dropped her. The brunette's mind slowly began to focus and what she saw made her blood run cold. The principal, Remus, had Cait in a headlock, but it didn't last long. The redhead had managed to escape it and lashed out at him in a blind rage.

"Mine!" The sound that left her mouth could only be described as animalistic. Cait's teeth had elongated and her ears were pointed. Snow also saw that her nails had grown to points as the woman slashed at Remus, ripping his suit. Mary was suddenly beside her, helping her stand.

"Are you okay, Snow?"

The girl nodded, but she didn't feel okay. She simultaneously felt hot and cold. What had she been about to do? It had happened so fast she wasn't even really sure. "What happened?"

"I'm so sorry. I don't really believe in interrupting a mating ritual, but I felt it was necessary, since you're human. When I told Remus what was about to happen, he said we needed to stop you two."

Snow couldn't help the irritation that filled her even if she didn't entirely understand where it came from. "Why?"

Mary gave her a pitying look. "Have you ever seen an alpha werewolf mate with their imprint for the first time?"

Snow shook her head.

"Let's just say that their mates take some damage if there isn't an omega to oversee the ritual. Really, it's only the first time that's bad. After that, her human side will gain control and I'm happy to say, most have a healthy sex life." The leopard smiled at her blush.

Another snarl ripped through the air as Cait sank her teeth into Remus's shoulder. Mary winced.

"I always knew Cait was strong, but I had always thought Remus was stronger. It doesn't look like that now," Mary mumbled.

The brunette looked over to the two werewolves and Cait seemed to have the upper hand, if Remus's bloody leg and shoulder were anything to go by. Remus managed to get out from under her jaws and slashed at Cait's chest, drawing blood.

"Will she be okay?" Snow felt dread in her gut at the sight of the woman's blood.

"I don't know. When a mating ritual is interrupted, it's a guaranteed fight to the death."

Snow's head jerked to meet her gaze. "They're going to kill each other?"

Mary shook her head. "Normally they would, but Remus called his pack. I think he did it as a precaution, though. I think he thought he could handle Cait. It's a good thing he called for backup. Now, he just has to survive until they get here."

Snow shuddered. "What happens if he can't?"

Mary frowned. "Let's just hope he does."

"Why don't they shift? I heard werewolves preferred to fight in wolf form."

"We're in your apartment. They wouldn't even fit in here. They might tear down the whole building."

"They get that big?"

"I take it you've never seen a shifted werewolf?"

Snow shook her head.

"Let's just say they are big enough."

Suddenly there was a whimper, and Snow looked over to the battlers to see Remus on his knees. Cait had her hand buried deep in his shoulder. She looked monstrous but beautiful. The ding of the elevator was heard just as Cait raised her clawed hand, ready to plunge it into his chest. The sound of several pairs of footsteps was heard as her hand descended. She was tackled to the ground by two burly men that could easily be linebackers. Her hand left Remus's shoulder with a sickening, wet, plopping sound as the two men body-slammed her into the ground. Two women were close behind and paused by their alpha, who was gripping his shoulder. Blood fell from the gash on the side of his head into his left eye.

Remus gasped out, "Help them; she's in a blind rage, but she's strong."

The two women nodded and helped the two men hold Cait to the ground. The redhead struggled, wildly thrashing, and several times she nearly got free. Snow wondered what their plan was. Were they going to just wait until she wore herself out? The girl looked at the redhead. That didn't look to be happening anytime soon. She just looked like she was getting more pissed off.

The elevator dinged again and another woman came running down the hallway. She wasn't as tall as any of the previous werewolves, and she looked less muscular. Her hair was a light blond that was pulled up into a messy bun. The woman ran over to where they were holding down Cait, and after one confirming look from Remus, she dove on top of the redhead, landing on her chest. She placed both her hands on either side of Cait's head and forced the woman to look in her eyes. Cait suddenly stilled and the fight seemed to leave her.

Snow whispered, "Who is that?"

"That is Gwen, their omega."

# CHAPTER FIVE

Gwen held Cait's gaze and spoke in soothing tones, "I'm sorry we interrupted you."

"Mine!"

"I know, I know she's yours, but you would have hurt her."

Cait whimpered. "No. Hurt."

"It's okay, though. She's okay."

"No, hurt?"

"I promise we won't hurt her, and you didn't either."

"Mine."

"Yes, she is yours."

"Not mine."

Gwen paused and without looking away from Cait, she called out for Snow. "Bring the girl to me. Move slowly."

Mary began to lead Snow over to them when suddenly a growl ripped out. "Not hers!"

"Mary, let her come by herself."

Mary nodded and gave Snow a gentle nudge. The girl slowly walked over to them and waited.

"Come down here," Gwen said softly, and Snow kneeled

down next to them, in between the two men that were holding Cait's arms down.

"I need you to reassure her."

Snow looked puzzled. "How?"

"She's lost to her wolf. I need you to speak with her wolf. I can only calm her; I can't bring her back. I need you to reason with them."

"I don't know how."

"You can start by touching her."

Snow hesitated but slowly reached out and let her hand make contact with Cait's cheek. The wolf seemed to lean into her touch.

"Mine?"

It was asked like a question. She didn't know how to respond. Only moments ago she had been so sure of her answer, but in the heat of the moment. After the vicious display, she was scared. Scared of the power the woman in front of her could wield. Scared of who she could hurt.

Gwen laid her hand on top of Snow's. The girl immediately felt a wave of calmness flood her. Among the calmness, she felt something hot and spicy mixed in. It wrapped around her and made her feel safe and loved. She met Gwen's gaze and whispered, "What is that?"

"Those are her feelings. She can't articulate them right now because the wolf is in control, but that is what she feels for you."

"I don't understand."

Cait whimpered, and Snow found herself rubbing her cheek softly. The woman relaxed slightly.

"I don't understand them."

Gwen nodded. "You don't have to. Right now, she just needs assurance."

"But, I don't know if I can give that to her."

"You are her imprint, right?"

"Her what?" Snow asked.

Gwen looked startled. "Don't you know?"

Snow shook her head. "I don't know what that means. What is an imprint?"

Gwen looked back to Remus, who had already begun to heal. The hole was still in his shoulder, but the gash on the side of his head had sealed. "Remus, why doesn't she know anything? What clan does this woman come from?"

Remus grunted. "Fallon's clan."

Gwen's face paled, and Cait began to become restless. "No wonder," she mumbled before turning back to Snow. "Well, I guess we have to do this the hard way then."

"What's the hard way?"

Gwen smiled cheerily. "I'm going to need you to kiss her if you can't vocalize it."

Snow's cheeks immediately turned red. "What?"

"It's just a kiss, but it will be enough at this stage."

"But—"

"Will you let her verbally claim you? Will you submit?"

Snow shook her head in confusion.

"Then a kiss will suffice."

Snow pulled her hand back from Cait's cheek and the werewolf began to move as she watched the two women go back and forth. She was beginning to get irritated.

"I don't know."

Gwen sighed in exasperation. "Well, you have to give her something. She's sworn herself to you for eternity..." Gwen trailed off as she saw Snow becoming more and more pale as she spoke.

"Just think about it as the equivalent of saying, I'll think about it."

Snow still looked uncertain, so Gwen tried a new tactic.

"You like this woman, right?"

"Cait," Snow mumbled.

"What?"

The brunette looked up. "She's not just some woman. Her name is Cait."

Gwen smiled. Now they were getting somewhere. "I'm sorry. You like Cait, right?"

Snow blushed.

"Don't you want her to go back to normal?"

"Because her wolf is in control right now?"

Gwen nodded. "Her wolf won't relinquish control until you give it your answer. Even if it's just a maybe. It needs to be reassured."

"A kiss will be enough?"

"For now, yes. It will do."

Snow looked down at Cait, whose once electric-blue eyes were now gold, and seemed more wild than usual as they bore into her own.

"Mine?"

Snow smiled and placed her hand back on the woman's cheek. She slowly leaned down until she was just hovering above Cait's lips. It's just a maybe. It shouldn't hurt, right? She closed the distance. The kiss was just a soft, light touching of lips. Cait's lips were supple, even though they looked so hard. She pressed more firmly into the wolf, suddenly needing the reassurance that she didn't mind the kiss. Suddenly, there was a gentle hand on her own cheek and Cait pressed into the kiss. Snow felt warmth flood her as well as the hot and spicy feeling she had felt earlier. It was intoxicating, and she found herself deepening the kiss, wanting to feel more.

Cait's hand guided her closer and the girl felt the warm tip of the wolf's tongue slide against the seam of her lips.

She hesitated at first, but when the tongue asked for entrance again, she felt a sudden boldness and opened her mouth to accept the woman. Cait wasn't polite upon entry. She immediately dominated Snow's mouth as if she was trying to claim it as her own. When their tongues touched, Snow let off a low moan at the silky feeling as they dueled for dominance.

Snow's other hand framed Cait's face and stroked it softly as they moved against one another. She wanted to touch more of the woman. She wanted to be touched. Those thoughts startled her and she pulled out of the kiss, needing air. She rested her forehead against Cait's as she panted. When she met the woman's striking blue eyes, she saw they looked more human. The wildness was still there, but it looked subdued. Cait's gaze had softened. She was back.

Snow moved back to give the werewolf some space. The brunette didn't know when the other werewolves had let go of Cait but she was now in a sitting position, as Gwen had moved off of her chest. Cait smiled at her, causing the brunette to blush and tuck a strand of chestnut hair behind her ear. "You're back?"

Cait nodded. "I am."

"Hi."

The werewolf chuckled. "Hello."

"I hate to break up the happy reunion, but we should probably move from the hallway," Gwen said as she helped Remus stand. He staggered but nodded.

"Cait, we need to talk."

Cait sighed, unrepentant of what she had done. "I know."

She stood and held out her hand for Snow to take. The girl smiled and accepted it, allowing herself to be led back into her small, two-bedroom apartment. All the werewolves filed in after them, along with Mary. She wasn't going to miss out on all this action.

Cait and Snow sat down on the loveseat while one of the male werewolves pulled a chair over for Remus and Gwen.

The blond smiled at him. "Thank you, Sam."

"My pleasure, Gwen."

Remus sighed as he sat and waited for everyone to get comfortable. He cleared his throat and began.

# CHAPTER SIX

"I would like to start by saying that, I'm sorry, to you Cait. What I did was..." he trailed off.

She sneered, "Stupid?"

Remus nodded. "Yes, it was stupid, but I believed it was necessary. I hope you can forgive me."

Snow interrupted. She was officially confused. "Why are you saying sorry? You were the one to get attacked."

Gwen decided to answer that one. "A mating ritual between a werewolf and their imprint is sacred. When Remus interrupted, he indirectly challenged Cait for the right to have you, even if that wasn't his intention."

"I'm confused."

Gwen nodded. "I can understand that. I take it neither of you are really aware of imprinting, or the mating ritual, or you wouldn't have engaged so quickly without the proper precautions?"

Cait growled before huffing and looked away while crossing her arms. "It would have been fine," she mumbled.

"No, it wouldn't have. You were out of control Cait. The wolf completely took over!" Remus yelled.

"I said it would have been fine!" she yelled back.

Gwen stood between the two of them breaking their eye contact. They both growled but Gwen cut them off. "That's enough."

Then she turned to Cait. "You obviously have never seen an alpha mate if you think it would have been fine." She turned to Remus. "And you aren't her alpha, so quit trying to subdue her. She's obviously stronger than you and I know she is older."

"She just got lucky."

Cait snorted.

Gwen sighed. "Spoken like a true alpha. We came here to talk. So, let's talk. Keep your teeth in your mouths and your claws in your laps."

Sam snorted. "Good luck with that."

Gwen ignored him and took her seat. "Remus, I don't know the full situation. Why don't you begin with what you have to say?"

"My offer still stands."

Cait snarled at him. "I will not submit to you!"

Gwen sighed. "You know what? How about I start this conversation. Cait, I don't know you but I know werewolves. Not only am I one, but I have overseen many mating rituals in my lifetime, what I know is from experience. So, when I say it would have ended badly had you continued, please try to believe me."

"I wouldn't have hurt her."

"Not intentionally."

"Not ever."

Gwen answered patiently as if speaking with a child. "Have you ever seen a blood bond?"

Cait paused but shook her head.

"Do you know how to consciously do one?"

"I would have figured it out."

Remus gave a bitter laugh. "And probably killed the poor girl in the process!"

Cait growled and was on her feet in minutes. Gwen was standing between them, and Snow had stood, and was gripping Cait's arm tightly. The brunette didn't know how she anticipated the werewolf's movement but her body had moved before her mind caught up. She had just felt the sizzle of anger as if it were her own. This was all really beginning to scare her.

Gwen looked at the couple in puzzlement before meeting Cait's glare. "Take a seat."

"Please Cait. I don't want anyone to get hurt anymore," Snow pleaded.

Cait relaxed and resumed her seat next to her mate. She threw her arm around Snow's waist pulling the girl securely into her. Snow all but melted into her, resting her head on the werewolf's shoulder. She felt exhausted.

Gwen sat back down. The look of puzzlement deepening. Remus sighed. "Do you see what I mean Gwen. This is dangerous. The bond is advancing too quickly."

Gwen nodded. "How long have you two known each other? A year?"

Cait nuzzled Snow's hair causing the girl to relax further into her. "Snow just met me today."

"A day? You've only know each other for one day? You're lying!"

Remus shook his head. "No, they're not Gwen. Snow just transferred to Monster High today. Cait is her homeroom teacher. To my knowledge, they've only known each other for a day."

"That's impossible."

"What's the problem?" Cait asked annoyed.

Gwen ignored her. “Is it because she’s a Fallon? Much of that clan’s history is a secret, especially their mating ritual.”

Remus shook his head. “I don’t know. All I know is that this is dangerous for the both of them.”

“Are you going to answer me or what?”

Gwen turned back to her. “Forgive me Cait, but this is just so surprising.”

“Why?” Snow asked.

“The bond that I feel coming from you two is strong. Not as strong as a blood bond but—”

Remus interrupted, “Why don’t you explain it from the beginning, Gwen.”

Gwen nodded. “Right, I’m sorry. Let me explain the mating ritual so you can understand.”

Cait and Snow nodded.

“As you know, the ritual begins with a touch. Just making eye contact or anything nonphysical isn’t enough. The two mates have to have a physical contact of some type. I heard it described as an electric shock or burning heat of some type.”

“We had that,” Cait said.

“After that, the two mates begin the courting. You have to understand that just because the werewolf imprints on someone doesn’t mean there is instant love or need for intimacy. Imprinting is simply the instance when a werewolf becomes completely devoted in every way to a person.”

“What do you mean?” Snow asked.

“What I’m saying is that, just because a werewolf imprints doesn’t mean the relationship the two people have will be sexual or marriage. It is simply the act of the werewolf swearing their life to the person for eternity. Some of the relationships remain platonic as really good friendships.”

"What about the blood bond?" Cait asked.

Gwen nodded. "What about it?"

"Doesn't it have to do with sex?"

Gwen shook her head. "You really don't know anything. And I say that in the nicest way possible. But no, a blood bond doesn't have to involve sex. It does, however, have to happen for the to mates to survive. I know you're confused but let me keep explaining. Once the werewolf imprints, the courting begins. It is during this phase when the two mates decide what type of relationship they will commit to. It ends when the imprintee either accepts or denies the werewolf's commitment."

"Denies it?" Snow asked.

Gwen's features darkened. "It's rare but sometimes the imprintee denies the werewolf. It's very tragic. The wolf doesn't last long afterward. They either go insane or kill themselves.

Snow gasped at the realization of what could have happened to Cait, had she not kissed her, sunk in. Her insecurities had almost killed the woman she was currently cuddled into. She was finally beginning to understand why the mating ritual was so dangerous for the both of them. She snuggled even closer into Cait and gripped the woman's t-shirt tightly. She didn't know if she loved Cait but she definitely didn't want her to die. Her heart ached at the thought.

"How long does the courting usually take?" Cait asked.

"Usually anywhere from one to five years. It's a big commitment for both parties and it takes them time to decide the relationship they want. They have to get to know each other. It's like blind dating. They usually don't even know the person they imprint on, all they know in the beginning is that they suddenly belong to this person for the rest of their life, and werewolves live a long time as you know."

Cait nodded. She couldn't say she was shocked at that information but at the same time she was more connected to Snow than she was willing to let on. Though, she didn't think she would ever imprint on the girl. This was indeed a turn of events. At least, this would make it easier to keep her promise from all those years ago.

"What about the blood bond? What is that?"

Gwen nodded. "It's the devotions of both the werewolf and their mate to each other. The full acceptance on both parts. It can go one of two ways, but both require some guidance from the wolf's clan, either from the alpha or the omega. One way is a blood bond of lovers, and the other is the blood bond of friends. Obviously, the lover's bond is committed during the act of sex."

"What happens exactly?"

"In both, the werewolf completes the bond by marking their mate. By biting them."

Cait frowned. "That's it?"

"It's a bite from the wolf. It hurts like fuck or so I'm told."

Cait shivered. Did that mean she had to transform completely into her wolf to commit the bond? Now that surprised her.

Gwen continued. "That's not the full extent of it though. The problem comes in when the imprintee is supposed to submit."

"Submit?" Snow asked through a yawn.

Gwen nodded. "If the imprintee has any doubt during that moment when the wolf bites them, the wolf will sense it."

"What happens then?" she asked, a sinking feeling settling in her gut.

"I'm sorry but the nature of a werewolf isn't pretty. If the imprintee has any doubt during the bond the werewolf will sense it and eat them."

"Eat them," Snow repeated.

"Yes."

"Like put them in their mouth, chew them up, and swallow them?" she rambled.

Gwen nodded. "Werewolves are animals, Snow. We are half human, but at the end of the day, we are monsters as well."

Snow shuddered. She couldn't even think of Cait eating her. She always felt so safe in the woman's presence despite only knowing her for a day. Despite her discomfort at that information, she was beginning to submit to the warmth emitting from Cait, and her eyelids felt heavy. *She would just close them for a minute.* Remus cut in. His voice holding an air of arrogance that grated on Cait's nerves. The man had always been reliable to her, but whenever he felt he had one leg up on her, he wasn't afraid to show it. "So, you understand now? Why I had to stop you?"

Cait nodded. "I do."

"So you'll—"

She cut him off, "Still, I will not submit to you. You will never be my alpha, Remus. I will never belong to any other clan other than that of Fallon."

"You can't be serious!" he yelled.

"I am."

"You'll wait until you kill her? Then what? You either go insane or kill yourself? You're the last Fallon. Do you want to end your bloodline in such a dishonorable way!"

Cait waited until he was done. She had managed to gain

more control over her temper, now that she understood the situation better, and that Snow had accepted her no matter how tentatively. She felt like her axis had been restored and she was fully back in control of her wolf.

"Say what you will Remus. I've made my decision."

Gwen pleaded with her. "Won't you please reconsider, Cait? I'd hate to see another tragedy? You two have progressed so fast but I fear without the right guidance you won't be able to handle the bond."

Cait paused to think all of this over. She wouldn't ever submit to another alpha. Her wolf wouldn't let her. Not after what had happened in her past. But how could she protect Snow from herself?

"Would you be willing to help me, Gwen?"

"I would be honored to help the last Fallon to mate!"

"Even if I didn't join your clan?"

Gwen paused and a snarl ripped from Remus's mouth. "Never! She is my omega and I won't let her."

"I was speaking to Gwen. To my understanding, the omega isn't subdued by the alpha's power of subjugation. She only listens to you through loyalty, not power."

Remus was at a loss for words. This was one thing Cait was sure of from her memories as a child. The omega of her clan was the weakest but she was free of the alpha's command. She had witnessed her father and their omega fight over things on several occasions. Her father had secretly loved the verbal battles and had always made Cait part of them as her lessons to learning how to be an alpha, and therefore the next leader of the Fallon Clan. She felt the familiar sting in her chest that always came from thinking about her clan. It had lessened over time but it would never disappear.

"Will you, Gwen."

The omega spent a long moment thinking it over as Remus rambled on about how she would never do it. Gwen didn't know Cait or Snow, but she had felt the link when she was connected to the both of them. It was stronger than anything she had ever felt. She had kept her cool during the situation, as was her way, but she had been full of fear. The power of Cait's wolf was massive.

She had never felt anything so dark and ancient. What she did know was that Cait hadn't fully lost control over her wolf. She had been restraining the bulk of it. Only a small part of her had given into it. Gwen had felt the struggle for dominance between the beast and the woman. It had terrified her. It had burned her when she tried to push deeper into the link she had established.

Honestly, getting Snow to call Cait back and give the woman the edge she needed over the wolf, was the only thing she could think to do. She knew that at any moment, Cait would have massacred them all without a second thought, despite the wolf not being entirely in control. Gwen had felt her own wolf submitting to its better. The woman was a true alpha. Probably, the strongest she had ever had the pleasure of meeting. If Snow and Cait went through the blood bond, and there was no question that they would, then they would need help.

Truthfully, she was excited at the prospect of helping the last Fallon continue the line of one of the greatest clans to have ever existed. Not only that, but her own wolf was intrigued by the ancient wolf it had brushed up against only moments before, and she herself was intrigued by the bond. It seemed she had already made up her mind.

Gwen cut Remus off mid sentence with her quietly spoken reply, "I'll do it."

Cait smiled while Remus sputtered. "You will not!"

"Remus, I love you like the friend that you are and even though you are my alpha you don't control me. I follow you of my own will. I'm going to do this whether you like it or not."

She turned back to Cait. "I'll do it but I don't think either of you are ready yet in my professional opinion. Despite the bond between you two forming so quickly, Snow is still human and you saw how she hesitated with just kissing you. She needs time to sort out her feelings, to get to know you. Even though she has accepted your courting, she never had the chance to decide what kind of relationship she wanted with you. She was just acting on her own instincts, though human as they are."

Cait nuzzled into the girl's hair. Snow had fallen asleep. "She's not human. Or at least not a full human."

Gwen looked genuinely surprised. "A half-blood then?"

Cait nodded. Remus cut in. "I wondered about that as well. Did she tell you what she was?"

Cait hesitated, then shook her head. Her past and how it involved Snow wasn't something she wanted just anyone to know, and despite how well she knew Remus, she still didn't trust him completely. He wouldn't hesitate to use the information against her if it meant he could control her. He wasn't evil, just young and stupid. He didn't know the fire he was trying to play with. He would learn in time.

"So what should we do?" the redhead asked.

Gwen thought a moment. "You're her teacher?"

Cait nodded.

"How old is she?"

"She just had her eighteenth birthday a few days ago."

Gwen cooed, "She's so young."

Cait smiled. "She's old enough."

"Well, how do you think you'll handle her being around

other people that might possibly try to court her? Do you think you'll kill any suitors for trying to get her attention?"

Cait growled and Snow snuggled into her tugging on her shirt. The werewolf immediately calmed before answering. "I'll manage. I think."

"I guess that's the best I can get from you, but if it starts to become dangerous for either of you, I would recommend you use your vacation time. Just until the blood bond is complete. After that, your wolf will be more manageable, though not entirely immune to jealousy."

Cait nodded and stood, carefully picking up Snow in her arms, as if she weighed nothing. The girl frowned until she was securely against Cait's chest again, to which she quickly buried her nose into the woman's neck.

"Well, I don't see anything else we need to talk about or at least nothing that can't wait until tomorrow. I'm tired and it's late."

Gwen hesitated before asking the question she had been dreading asking since she realized they were running out of things to talk about. "Will you be sleeping here?"

Cait paused as if she had suddenly realized the situation. "I..."

"I'm not saying you can't. Believe me when I say I understand, but if you're going to stay here then I would like to invite myself over for the night as well. For safety of course. I would also recommend that you sleep on the couch."

Cait huffed. "For safety?"

"Of course." Gwen smiled.

"I don't think I can leave if I'm being honest."

"Then I can stay?"

"Yeah. I would like that."

Remus muttered as he and the other werewolves filed

out of the apartment. The two other women hugged Gwen before leaving, and the two other men sent her a nod of respect, before following Remus out. The alpha left in a huff and didn't even say goodbye. Cait didn't blame him. She had made his wolf submit to her own and she had scared it even if the man was fascinated by the power. Men like Remus could be dangerous if they weren't managed correctly. He may not be in her clan, but she knew how to manage his type. She had met many like him in her past. Men that wanted to claim the power of a Fallon for their own. She would never submit again.

# CHAPTER SEVEN

When Snow woke, it was to an empty feeling. It wasn't the usual kind of empty that let her know she needed to eat breakfast, but the empty feeling that made her feel like something was missing. She yawned and stood from her bed after pushing the covers away. Despite having just woke she still felt exhausted. What had happened yesterday? She wondered as she left her bedroom. The brunette didn't remember climbing into bed. The empty feeling lessened as she came closer to the living room, and her heart skipped a beat when her brown eyes settled on the woman sleeping on her couch. The woman's mane of red locks was mused into a bird's nest that she was sure her own mirrored, and the werewolf was sleeping in her bra, along with a pair of booty shorts with the word, 'Pink,' written across the ass. She was sleeping on her stomach and must have gotten hot in the middle of the night as she had kicked the blanket off.

Snow couldn't help being struck by the beauty the woman on her couch exuded. Every cell in the brunette's body called for her to move forward and touch the redhead as if she as a moth being called to the flame. She found herself moving towards the woman, and before she could stop the curiosity of wanting to see if the tan flesh was as soft as it looked, she ran her fingers lightly along Cait's spine. The werewolf's skin erupted in goosebumps, and Snow knew her own ability to turn things into ice, and being able to freeze things, was leaking out of her. Her hands must have become colder as she touched Cait, but the woman was so hot, and she wanted to feel the heat cover her. Surround her. She splayed her hand across the werewolf's back and trailed it down the woman's spine again, this time getting a real feel of the softness of her skin. The warmth shot straight up her arm and settled comfortably in her chest. Cait mumbled and made a move to turn over. Promptly falling off the couch.

Snow giggled as she watched the werewolf look around confused as to what had happened. Snow stopped laughing when the redhead's electric blue orbs settled on her and filled with mischief. The girl didn't have a chance as the woman tackled her to the ground, cushioning their fall, and flipped the brunette over so she straddled her waist.

"That wasn't very nice," Cait growled.

"I didn't do anything."

"Yes you did, and now I'm going to punish you." Cait grinned as she lifted her hands.

Snow shivered. "How?"

"Like this!" Suddenly, fingers were tickling her down her sides, and Snow laughed uncontrollably as she tried to fend off the onslaught from her attacker.

"Sto— Stop— I can't— stop!"

"I can't hear you. You have to speak louder," Cait sang

as she continued her attack. Cait's hands wandered until she hit a soft spot down Snow's side, the girl let out a moan of pleasure. Cait paused and touched the spot again, slowly. It was between the girl's left breast and her first rib. Snow moaned again. Her face flushed, and her eyes closed as her whole body tensed. The redhead couldn't stop herself. The girl beneath her was too irresistible, and she longed to elicit more sounds from her. She bent down and captured Snow's lips. At first, the girl was unsure, but the warmth from the woman above her lured her in. The brunette found herself responding to the kiss, to the feeling behind it, and to the way it made her feel as if she was irresistible. She slanted her mouth against Cait's to try and take control, and when the werewolf asked for entrance, Snow denied it. Cait trailed her fingers down to the sensitive spot eliciting a gasp, Cait entered her mouth, claiming it. Their tongues slid against each other and Snow found herself giving into the feelings and the heat. She moaned again and deepened the kiss.

A loud clanging sound rang out cutting through the daze the couple had found themselves in. Cait growled as she jerked away from Snow to meet the perceived threat only to stop when her gaze met Gwen's. The blond woman was smiling while holding a pot and the spatula she had been banging against it to make the sound. Snow groaned and hid her face in embarrassment behind her hands.

"Time to get ready for school!" Gwen sang, and she banged the pot a few more times for added effect.

Cait sighed, climbed off of Snow, and stood helping the embarrassed girl to her feet. "We better get ready. We don't want to be late to class," she admitted begrudgingly.

The brunette could only nod and watch as Cait went to her duffel bag, pulling out some clothes from it, before heading to the bathroom. How the woman knew her way around her apartment she wasn't sure, but she couldn't find it in herself to mind?

"Come on Snow. You need to get ready as well. Cait said the bus comes at seven thirty and it's already seven. You still need to eat breakfast and brush your teeth," Gwen chirped as she ushered the girl back towards her bedroom. Snow couldn't help her cheeks flushing in embarrassment. Her skin was so pale it was impossible to hide.

"Make sure you change your underwear!" Gwen sang out as she retreated down the hallway and Snow erupted in a full body flush. Why couldn't a hole just open up in the ground and swallow her whole? She wondered as she pulled open her panty drawer.

To say homeroom was awkward was an understatement. Snow could feel Cait's presence as if it was part of her no matter where she went. It didn't help that people kept giving her strange looks as she walked down the hallway. She didn't understand it. She knew that Cait was back in homeroom as she walked to her next morning class. The brunette could feel exactly where the woman was at all time, but at the same time, she also felt like the werewolf was with her, as if part of the werewolf had become part of her own being.

I'll have to ask Gwen about it later, she thought. Snow also couldn't help feeling like a cold glare was following her throughout the day as well. It felt like it was boring holes through her wherever she went, but every time she glanced around, no one was paying attention to her. Well, besides the puzzled looks she kept getting from the more animalistic monsters, like the kitsune and the dog demons. She sniffed her clothing a few times but she smelt like she always did, though there was a softer smell of rainwater that she knew to be Cait's, that clung to her as well.

By the time lunch had rolled around she was beginning to get really annoyed of the stares and whispers. She snapped at a dog demon as he sniffed while walking past her to the lunch line.

"Do I smell or something?"

The boy looked startled but paused to study her for a moment. "Not really."

"Then why do people keep sniffing me and staring at me?"

His face scrunched up. "You kind of smell funny."

"What? Like what?"

He thought for a minute before answering. "You smell dangerous."

Snow frowned. "What?"

"Yeah, you smell like power. An old power. It's hard to explain, but my instincts are telling me to be careful around you."

"Oh."

The boy frowned then proceeded to cut her in the lunch line. Snow frowned but decided to let him. She didn't want to start a fight. It would turn out bad for whoever she fought because she was sure Cait would step in whether she was close by, or whether she had to run from the teacher's lounge to help her. Snow frowned. This was all so crazy, and it was happening so fast. Like lightning fast. She barely had time to think it all through.

She never imagined that a rebellious act of transferring schools, so she could experience the high school life that her parents had, would lead to her being pursued by a werewolf. The thing that scared her the most was that she didn't mind that Cait was pursuing her. Actually, it made her feel really good. It was like having a loyal friend alway close by. Someone she could count on or turn to no matter what, someone that would love her unconditionally. The brunette had never felt such a strong connection to someone.

Snow never admitted it to her parents, but she had never really fit in at her old school. The other monsters had given her a wide berth. She had just thought it was because of who her grandmother was, but after yesterday when that harpy attacked her, leaving a gash on her head as she called her a half-blood, she was beginning to wonder if they had made her an outcast due to something else. The girl didn't know what a half-blood was exactly. She hated to admit it, but she had been home-schooled most of her life as her parents were extremely protective of her. The brunette reached up to touch the gash, that would probably leave a scar, only to feel smooth skin where it had been. Confused, she ran her hand along the other side of her face. Nothing.

Snow ran out of the lunchroom, her heart in her throat, and into the first bathroom, she came across, going straight to the mirror. She gazed confused at her reflection. It was gone. The gash was gone. When had it healed? She didn't have supernatural healing powers. She could only control ice and the cold. Otherwise, she was basically human. Snow had a frown on her face as she left the bathroom only to bump into someone. Catching her balance on the wall, she looked up to apologize, only to have the words catch in her throat. It was the boy from yesterday. The one with red eyes. The vampire.

He stared at her, studying her. The brunette had the vague feeling that this had been the cold gaze she had felt following her all day. She shuddered as her heartbeat picked up.

"Your name is Snow." It was a statement.

She didn't answer.

"You are human."

Another statement.

He studied her with his cold gaze. Almost like a scientist would look into a microscope.

"You don't scare me."

This puzzled her. "What?"

"I was warned about you and your dog. I'm not scared of either of you," he said as he advanced on her, and pushed her up against the wall. Snow's heart was pounding in her chest. She was afraid it would burst from the cavity if it didn't slow down. This boy was dangerous. Everything inside of her wanted to lash out. She could feel the temperature dropping around them, and a thin layer of frost coated the hand he reached out to touch her neck with.

"Cute trick, but I could break your neck in a second if I wanted to."

Snow shuddered.

"I won't. Not because I was told to simply watch you, but because it would ruin the game, and I do love a good game. When you're ready, and it will be soon, we will move our first piece. A pawn perhaps. I'm the knight. You have to earn my tortures. Both of you do. But let me warn you that I won't ever let you reach the king or queen. You and your dog are unworthy of such an honor. I don't care what the good book says. I will be the one to end the both of you."

The boy stood back and sneered at her. He wiped the frost off of his hand and walked down the hallway leaving Snow to sag down the wall. She was so confused. Who was that boy? Why did he say those things? What did he mean?

Snow couldn't help the sting of tears that burned a trail down her cold cheeks. The connection told her that Cait was getting closer and quickly. She wanted the woman, and she wanted the werewolf to make her feel safe again, she wanted Cait.

## CHAPTER
# EIGHT

Cait refused to let Snow go home by bus. Instead, she drove her back to the girl's apartment, and once there, she refused to leave her side.

"Cait, I'm fine now. You can go home," Snow said from where she sat on the loveseat. Cait wanted to sit next to the girl but didn't want to crowd her.

"I'll wait until Gwen gets here."

Snow frowned. "Are you going to spend the night again? You don't have to. I'll be fine."

"Tell me what happened at school."

"I told you what happened. I was startled that the gash from the harpy disappeared and when I left the bathroom some jerk knocked me down in the hallway."

Cait studied her carefully. She wasn't stupid. She had smelt vampire on her mate. Not just any vampire. A dark blood. The worst kind of vampire. They practiced dark magic and tended to torture their prey before killing them. Cait especially despised dark bloods. Most people did, but with her it was personal. She crossed her arms over her chest and just stared at her mate, willing her to tell the whole truth.

"Cait you can go—" A knock at the door interrupted them. The werewolf smiled and stood up. Gwen greeted her when she opened the door.

"Good evening girls! I brought movies and popcorn. I thought we could have a movie night now that's it's finally the weekend."

Cait smiled and led the other werewolf into the living room.

"We can do that, but first, I need you to help me."

"With what?" Gwen looked between the two women. "Did something happen at school?"

"Smell her."

The blonde looked puzzled before taking a deep breath. She gasped and moved to get closer to the girl. "Are you okay? You're not hurt, are you? Did he hurt you? What happened at school?"

Snow fended off the prodding fingers. "I'll tell you what I told Cait; I'm fine."

"So the dark blood didn't do anything to you? His scent is all over you," Gwen asked as her hands stilled.

"Dark blood?" the brunette asked as a sinking feeling filled her gut. So that's how Cait knew something had happened. She smelt it on her. It really was hard to hide things from a werewolf.

Gwen frowned. "You were really sheltered as a child weren't you?"

Snow blushed. "Well, excuse me!"

"It's not her fault. Her parents had to..." Cait trailed off as she realized what she had let slip.

Snow was the first to ask, "You know my parents?"

Cait shrugged and shifted from foot to foot. "Kind of. Who doesn't."

"You seem to know them personally," Gwen stated.

"I met them in passing."

"But what you just said made it sound like you knew them well," Snow asked. Suspicion was sneaking into her as doubt.

"Did you know them?" Gwen asked point blank.

Cait didn't want to lie. She wasn't above it, but she didn't want to lie to Snow. She needed to get the girl to trust her more.

She sighed. "Fine, yes, I know your parents. I know them very well actually."

"How?" Snow demanded.

"That's a little more complicated to answer, but the short answer is that I met them through your grandmother."

Snow frowned. She felt like there was something she was forgetting. Something her grandmother had told her a long time ago. She shook it off in favor of asking more questions. "How did you know my grandmother?"

"Now that is a very long story, and I don't feel like telling it right now. Maybe some other time."

Snow opened her mouth to protest, but Gwen turned to her. "Who is your grandmother, Snow? She must be very old to know Cait."

"When she was alive she was known as Lidia Bennett."

Gwen gasped and dropped down into a kneel. "I am truly among greatness. It is an honor."

Snow frowned. She would never become used to this reaction, despite it having occurred ever since she was little, it always made her uncomfortable. "Don't Gwen. You don't have to kneel to me. I moved here to get away from that. I'm just Snow here."

Gwen looked up puzzled. "But your Lidia Bennett's only grandchild. She ended the great war between monsters and humans."

"She was just my grandmother. I'm nothing great like her. What I want to know is how you know my family, Cait?"

"Why?"

"Are you a friend of my grandmother or my mother?"

"I guess you could say both. Though, I wouldn't call me much of a friend. I was more like a curse."

Something clicked in Gwen's mind as she thought Cait's words over, as well as the stories of the redhead, that had been passed down through Gwen's clan.

"Was she your savior?" Gwen suddenly blurted out, and both Snow and Cait looked to her.

"What?" Snow asked.

"I asked if she was the savior of the only Fallon survivor. Lidia the Benevolent. It was a story passed down through my clan about the Fallon's massacre."

Cait frowned. "You speak so lightly of it, but yes, she was the one that saved me on that night but at her own cost."

"If you know my grandmother and my mother did you know me before yesterday?" Snow wanted to know.

Cait sighed as she gave into her wolf and claimed the spot next to Snow on the loveseat. "Yes, you could say that. I met you only a few days after you had been born. It was one of the promises I had made to Lidia before you were born."

"What promises?"

"There were a few that I can't tell you, but the one that

deals directly with you was that I would protect you when the time came."

"What do you mean? Did you know you would imprint on her?" Gwen asked.

"No! Of course, I didn't. That was as much a surprise to me as it was to everyone else. Honestly, I don't know the full details of what Lidia knew. She was mysterious like that. She only ever gave a person enough information they needed to carry out their missions. I just remember that day. I was still lost. I went to Lidia for guidance. What she gave me helped me a little bit, but what she made me promise bound me to Snow.

She only told me at the time that I should live my life normally, but that a day would come when my path would cross her granddaughters', and at that time I would fulfill my promise to protect Snow even at the cost of my own life. That's all she told me. Your grandmother and I had a complicated relationship, but she always had the upper hand, and I trusted she always had my best interest at heart. That was the problem with ancient vampires like her. They always knew more than they let on, and they always knew more than you wanted them to."

Snow mulled all of this over. Exactly how old was the werewolf sitting next to her? Her grandmother was really old. So old, she had said she lost count centuries ago, and couldn't answer the question when Snow asked her on the woman's deathbed. Her grandmother had died when Snow was thirteen. Suddenly, the memory of a hot summer day with the old woman surfaced and the nagging feeling that she was forgetting something filled her. She let the feeling of nostalgia wash over her as she remembered.

Snow was ten and sat next to her grandmother out in the garden of their mansion. The woman always looked happy, and always exuded warmth and love, even though she was usually cold to the touch. Her mother said Snow had gotten her ability to freeze things from her grandmother, and the woman had recently begun to teach the small child how to control it. Occasionally, she would freeze things unintentionally.

"How are you, Snow?" Lidia asked.

"I'm good Gran." Snow grinned showing off her missing tooth. "The tooth fairy came last night and gave me five dollars."

Lidia chuckled. " That's good. I'm glad."

The two sat in silence for a moment. Snow loved her grandmother, but sometimes she never knew what to say to her. She always felt like she could say anything, but that she didn't need to say anything at all.

Lidia suddenly chuckled and Snow looked up at her. "Do you want me to tell you a story, Snow?"

"Okay."

Lidia cleared her throat and looked out unseeingly into the garden. "Once upon a time, there was a brave warrior."

"What was his name?" the little girl interrupted.

Lidia smiled down at her. "Her name was Cait Fallon. Now try not to interrupt and let me tell the story. You can ask all your questions at the end."

"Okay."

"Good. Now, where was I?"

"Cait!" the girl suggested.

"Ah, yes, Cait. Cait Fallon was a strong warrior, but she was missing something."

"What Gran?"

Lidia chuckled. "Cait was missing her heart."

Snow gasped. "Her heart?"

"That's right."

"But how does she breath?"

Lidia smiled. "Well, she had a real heart in her chest, but she was missing the heart in her soul."

Snow nodded sagely. "Oh, okay."

Lidia continued. "One day a man appeared and promised her he could give her what she needed, but at a price."

"What was that?"

"He asked that she give him her wolf, but only for a day."

"Wolf?"

Lidia nodded. "Cait was a werewolf. Do you know what that is?"

"Like Wolfgang."

"Well, Wolfgang is our pet, and he is just a dog. Cait is a werewolf. She's a lot bigger than Wolfgang."

"How big?"

Lidia looked around and glanced back at the mansion before she hummed. "Well, do you remember Uncle's Max's monster truck?"

"Yeah."

"She's about that big."

Snow's eyes widened. "That's really big."

Lidia smiled. "Indeed. Cait thought over this offer for a few days and returned to the man offering him her wolf for one day."

"What happened next?"

Lidia gave a sad smile. "The man used her wolf to hurt the people she loved the most."

Snow's face fell. "Why Gran?"

"That's a story for another time. Right now, I'm telling you the story of Cait."

"Okay."

"When Cait got her wolf back she was very sad, and to make it worse the man had lied to her, and couldn't give her what she wanted most."

"Her heart?"

"That's right."

"And one day a woman appeared to Cait and offered her something."

"Oh no."

"No, this woman was a kind woman and wanted to help Cait."

"What did she do?"

"She offered Cait, a job as her personal bodyguard. Cait couldn't refuse the offer because of who the woman was and slowly but surely Cait healed."

"Then what?"

"The woman had a vision one night and called Cait to her bedside. She made the werewolf make several promises, but the most important one was to protect a little girl that was going to be born in a few days."

"A little girl? Like me?"

"Just like you." Lidia accented it by poking Snow's nose. The little girl giggled.

"Why?"

"Because this little girl would be very important to Cait as well as many other people."

"What was her name?"

"That's a secret."

"Aw."

"Don't worry, one day you will know. Just be patient."

"Okay."

"Cait made the promise, and left to carry out the other promises, but not until she had seen the little girl's birth."

"Was Cait still sad?"

Lidia was surprised for a moment before she smiled. “Yes, Cait was still very sad, but she was stronger than ever before after carrying out the promises of the woman.”

“Then what?”

“For the rest, you will have to wait and find out.”

“Aw, why can’t you just tell me now?”

“Because the rest hasn’t happened yet and not even I can tell the future. I will tell you one thing.”

“What’s that?”

“The little girl would help Cait find her heart.”

“Her real one?”

“Yes, Snow. Her real one. And that would heal Cait’s pain so she wouldn’t be sad anymore.”

“I want to make Cait happy too. Can I be her friend?”

Lidia smiled as she stroked Snow’s hair. “I hope you will one day, Snow. I hope you will.”

# CHAPTER NINE

Snow gasped and stared at Cait as if she was seeing her for the first time. "You're Cait Fallon!"

The werewolf nodded slowly, worried that the girl had regressed during their conversation. "I think we've established that."

"No, what I mean is that you're the Cait Fallon that my grandmother was always telling me stories about."

"Stories?" Gwen asked.

Snow nodded as her features suddenly saddened. The memories of all the sad stories, that she had thought of as fairy tales of a strong and brave female werewolf, whom she had always secretly been rooting for, that her grandmother told her as a small child were all real. They were of how the werewolf would fight evil for the kind old woman who had saved her. The endings were always melancholy, but her grandmother would always remind Snow of that same story she had told to her on that hot summer day in the garden, and the girl would hope, and pray that the werewolf would one day find her heart.

As a little girl, she hadn't really understood what her

grandmother meant by the werewolf missing her heart. All she really understood was that the woman was sad and lonely and was missing something important. Even as she sat next to the redhead and gazed into her electric blue eyes, which were the windows into her soul, she could see the ever-present ache of loneliness. It reminded her of her own desire as a child to meet the werewolf of her stories, and give her a big hug.

"You're really Cait Fallon."

"What kind of stories did your grandmother tell you exactly? That woman had a way of making my life sound more heroic than it really was."

"But they were true, weren't they? You've been through so much," Snow felt her own heart ache as she spoke.

"I don't know what she told you, but I assure you I was far from heroic. For a time I was more like Lidia's personal soldier."

"What kind of things did she have you do?" Gwen asked.

Cait shrugged. "She usually sent me on missions of keeping the peace between the monsters and humans. I would find myself breaking up fights of ogres, trying to tear the heads off of annoying humans, or dark bloods using both monsters and humans as their playthings." Cait shuddered. "Those were never pleasant."

"But the stories—"

"I'm just me Snow. I'm nobody special. Not like you. I'm just a werewolf that has lived a long time and seen a lot, but I'm not a hero in any way."

Snow frowned. She was seeing a side of Cait that she knew she would never like. The self-pitying side of a century old werewolf who had made mistakes she didn't think she could right, no matter how many good things she did.

"I'll believe what I want to and I believe in the stories my gran told me as a child."

Cait sighed and stood. "Well, I'm not your boss nor do I control you, but I ask that you take what Lidia said with a grain of salt. She was a master storyteller and had a way about it that always made an average tale an epic adventure. So, how about that movie?"

Gwen stood up from the sofa she had sunk into and picked up the stack of Red Boxes that she had rented for the night, as well as the snacks she had brought over. "Who wants popcorn?"

SNOW HAD FALLEN asleep against Cait sometime after the second chick flick, and the werewolf had moved the girl to her bedroom before going out on the balcony. Cait breathed deeply and let the cool night air surround her, clearing her mind of the memories that had surfaced from the earlier conversation. She sighed when she heard Gwen follow her out.

"You can't change the seed that her grandmother planted no matter how hard you try. I would just give up and accept it." Gwen leaned her back against the rail and smiled at Cait.

"Lidia was alway planting seeds like that."

"I was told stories about you as well. Epic tales of honor and valor. I know most probably aren't true, but it doesn't stop the butterflies I get in your presence. I hate to say it, but I have some serious hero worship when it comes to people like you and Lidia."

Cait sighed. "Let's just get one thing straight. I'm not a hero. I never was, and I never will be. I'm the farthest thing from it. If I had to say I was anything, then I'm a curse."

"Why do you do that?"

"What?"

"Pity yourself like that? It's always in your scent. Your apathy. Has anyone ever told you that you smell like a thunderstorm? Powerful, wild, dangerous, but also sad and lonely."

Cait gazed out into the starless night. She missed the stars. "You don't know me well enough to demand those answers."

"Do you ever let anyone in Cait?"

"I used to. Sometimes. Maybe Lidia was the last one I ever will, and that's only because I owed her a great debt that I don't think I can ever repay. Why she trusted her granddaughter to me, I'll never know, but sometimes I think she made a mistake? Snow has many bodyguards and many people that would lay down their lives for her. She doesn't need someone like me."

"What? She doesn't need someone who would devote their eternity to her? I'll tell you this from what little experience I've had in my short life in comparison to yours. A werewolf's imprint is eternal. I don't mean that you devote yourself to Snow once and it's over. I don't know how old either of your souls are, but you both seem very old to me. So I feel like I can say this with confidence. You may have imprinted on her as a werewolf, but she is still your soulmate. You are two halves of one soul. Your souls have been seeking each other out lifetime after lifetime. Death after death. You have both been searching for one another. Whether you like it or not, you are her forever. You would never betray her because it would be like betraying yourself.

You think she would be better off with someone else? I can guarantee no one else could offer her the same devotion that her soulmate can. Lidia may have planted the seeds, but I feel like maybe she anticipated your imprint. Maybe what they said about her knowing the future was true. But at the end of the day, you have to make the decision to be there and protect Snow when she needs you most. Whether that is as a lover or a friend you two need to decide together but you know you will be there for her no matter what. You're her werewolf Cait. Start acting like it."

Gwen shoved off of the rail, moved to the sliding door, and slipped back into the apartment to get some sleep. Cait let Gwen's words wash over her. The woman might be a few centuries younger than her, but her words rang true. Cait sighed before standing straight. She couldn't deny the bond she had with Snow and truth be told she didn't want to. It was painful to try. For the both of them. To answer Gwen's earlier question, yes, she had been told she smelled like a thunderstorm. By Lidia. The ancient vampire had told her that when they first met, and she had pulled her bloody, bruised and broken, from the corpses of her kinsmen.

The corpses she had created through her own desire to stop the thunderstorm that had plagued her ever since her birth. Most had believed her scent turned that way after the massacre and chalked it up to pity, but the truth was that Cait had always smelt like a thunderstorm. Her mother had worried about it and had the medicine men of their clan look into it. The only answer they could come up with was one that Cait never really understood. The medicine men, as well as the clan elders, had told them that Cait had been born without heart. Her parents seemed to understand what the elders were saying, but no one ever explained it to her. All she knew was that as she aged and matured it was done with a great sadness that never seemed to leave her. It made the other children fear her. They said she smelt dangerous and strange. She could always smell the fear coming off them like a stink.

Her father had taken it upon himself to teach her what she would have normally learned from her peers. He taught her how to interact with others, soft skills, how to fight, and so on. He refused to have a weak alpha, as she was set to take over the clan, despite the complaints of the elders. They would say a wolf with no heart was dangerous. That she would be the death of the clan should she lead it. She proved them right when she only meant to find a cure. She had indeed killed them all. Cait suddenly felt very tired. She rubbed her eyes and with one last glance at the sky, retreated into the warmth of the apartment.

SNOW WOKE to the heavenly smell of bacon. Her stomach growled loudly, and the smell drew her from the bed, and into the kitchen where she found Gwen at the stove, and Cait leaning against the countertop making coffee. The two women had been speaking softly but stopped when Snow entered the kitchen. Cait smiled. “Morning Snow.”

“Morning.”

“Told you the bacon would do it. Works like a charm.” Gwen was way too cheery in the morning, Snow quickly decided, as she made her way to the kitchen table. It was just big enough for three people to sit at.

“Coffee or orange juice?”

"Juice? When did I get juice? Actually, when did I get bacon? I haven't shopped since moving here."

"You can thank Cait for that. She was up before even me and went shopping for us."

Snow smiled. "Thanks."

"It was nothing," she said as she filled a glass with orange juice and set it in front of the girl.

"So, what's on the agenda for today?" Gwen asked as she made up a plate of eggs, bacon, tomatoes, and toast, before setting it down in front of Snow. The brunette immediately dug in.

Cait smiled and turned to Gwen. They had both already eaten.

"I was planning on getting some grading done. I'm a little behind on my work. I'll need to go back to my apartment."

"Oh, well, you do have a real job. So, I guess it can't be helped."

Snow paused between mouthfuls. "What do you do Gwen?"

"Me? I'm a professional omega. I oversee mating rituals, childbirths, inter-clan disputes, you know, the works," she said as she took the seat across from Snow. The girl was already done eating and was chugging down her juice.

Cait asked, "I didn't know omegas were so busy."

"Yeah, well, werewolves have a temper problem as I'm sure you're aware of. They need someone to keep their human sides in control. Otherwise, more growling than talking happens, with the occasional bite."

"Sounds dangerous," Snow said as she moved to place her plate in the sink. Cait took it from her and washed the dish before sitting down at the table next to Snow.

"So I take it you have clan duties today?" Cait asked.

"You've guessed right. My schedule is packed this whole weekend."

"Will you still be able to come over in the evenings and stay the night?" Snow asked.

"Why? Want your werewolf close by you every night?" Gwen grinned as Snow blushed.

"I just like having Cait and you around."

"I'm sure you like have one of us around." Gwen chuckled as she stood.

Snow's blush deepened.

"Well kids, I have to hop to it. And to answer your question Snow, no, I won't be able to come over for the next couple of nights. I got a call this morning, and Remus has demanded that I come back. One of the females is giving birth to twins, and her husband is ready to kill something or someone. It's making the other wolves antsy. The baby is due within the week. The last week is always the hardest for the whole clan. But I'm sure you two will be alright. Cait's wolf has been fairly tame since what happened two nights ago, and I feel like I can trust it to behave itself until I come back."

"Okay." Snow frowned.

Gwen pointed at her. "I'm not saying you shouldn't be careful. No hanky panky while I'm gone. No lip locking or heavy breathing. Let sleeping dogs lie and all that."

Cait groaned. "Go Gwen. Remus sounded desperate."

"I mean it you two."

"Go already!"

Gwen chuckled and left the two in the kitchen. Cait heard the front door close and sighed. It really was nice having Gwen around. Her presence was calming, but the woman was too opinionated and way too happy. But Cait couldn't deny liking her. What could she say? The woman grew on her.

Snow interrupted her thoughts. “So, you're going back to your apartment?”

Cait nodded and stood. She walked over to the coffee pot and poured some into a to-go-mug that she had brought from her apartment the previous night. “Yeah, I've gotten behind on my work. I need to grade a few stacks of homework.”

“Oh, okay. Yeah, I have some homework I need to do as well.”

Cait turned around and smiled at Snow who had stood and was standing awkwardly in the middle of the kitchen. “Well, I better go.”

“Yeah.” Neither moved.

“Lots of work and stuff,” Cait mumbled.

“Mm-hmm.” Snow rocked back and forth on the balls of her feet.

“I'm going to just go...right now....” Cait trailed off as she watched Snow pull her bottom lip between her teeth and nod her head.

“Yeah.”

They moved in unison. Cait lifted Snow up onto the countertop as the girl wrapped her legs around the werewolf's waist. Their lips met with hunger and Snow let out a wanton moan as their tongues touched. Her body tingled all over. It had only been a day, but her body craved Cait's touch like a drug addiction. Cait's hands slipped under the girl's tank top. One splayed across the girl's back while the other began making circles on her stomach.

“Cait!”

“Yeah?”

“We can't--” She was cut off as their mouths met again.

"No?" The werewolf's hand traveled dangerously close to the brunette's breast. She slept braless.

Snow whimpered. "Touch me," she demanded.

Cait teased the edge of her breast but refused to give in. "What?" She smiled into the kiss.

"More."

"More what?" She drew circles around Snow's areola but refused to touch the nipples even though they had hardened.

"Please, Cait!" she begged.

Cait pulled back from the kiss which confused the girl, before Snow's head shot back banging against the cupboards. She groaned as Cait's hot mouth sucked her nipple in before biting it. Snow began to rub against the werewolves abs. Needing the friction to relieve the heat building between her legs.

"More."

"Where do you need me?" Cait grunted out as she felt her own control slipping. The wolf was waking up.

"Down there."

Cait's hand traveled lower but stopped at the girl's bellybutton. Her teeth teased the other nipple. "Guide me where you want me, baby."

Snow whimpered, and grabbed Cait's hand, but only gripped it tightly. Cait felt the girl flush in embarrassment.

"You can do it, baby. Guide me where you want me." She sucked the nipple before releasing it and meeting Snow's lips again. She rested her forehead against the girls.

"Come on. Show me," she whispered.

Snow nodded and met Cait's lips again. Slowly and hesitantly she guided the woman's hand lower until it rested on her hip.

"I know you want it lower than that."

Snow nodded again and inched their hands lower as if she didn't want to lose her nerve. They both groaned as Cait's hand met with the wet heat. She was so hot for her.

"Oh, Snow," Cait moaned. She could feel the wolf throwing itself against her mental cage. It was painful, but she wanted to go a little longer. She would stop before it became too dangerous, She thought as she rubbed against the girl's sex.

"Cait!" Snow moaned and moved her hips against the hand resting against her.

The wolf howled to mate. She needed to stop. Cait whimpered as pain erupted in both her chest and her head. She bit her lip as her whole body stilled.

"Cait?" Snow immediately felt the werewolf's tension but didn't understand it at first.

"Don't stop," she whined.

"I can't--" the woman said in clipped tones as if she was in pain.

"Can't what?"

Snow could feel the werewolf panting against her neck before she was suddenly alone in the room. Her mind was in a confused haze, and she didn't really know what happened until she heard the front door slam shut. She was suddenly cold and really pissed off at the same time. Why had Cait stopped?

# CHAPTER TEN

Cait didn't stop until she made it to the forest about a block away from Snow's apartment. She stripped with practiced ease and suddenly burst, releasing her wolf. Pain rippled through her entire body, and she let out a pained howl as she staggered on four legs drunkenly. Did she have phasing sickness? She vaguely wondered as she staggered into several trees knocking some over. Catching herself against one of the trees, she suddenly threw up. Her vision swayed from side to side. When was the last time she had phased? How many centuries? She had forgotten what it felt like. She didn't remember it being so painful. Cait staggered through the forest until she reached a lake and collapsed at the water's edge. Her tongue snaked out to desperately lap at the water that she could barely reach.

The werewolf felt like she had the flu. Every muscle ached. Her bones felt like they'd been broken and reformed, which she knew is what happened during the transformation, but it used to happen so seamlessly. It was her own fault. After the massacre, she had denied herself this. This union with her wolf. She feared what would happen. The wolf had been within her mental cage for so long that she had forgotten the feeling of the wind running through her white fur. The enhancement of her senses. She had forgotten the wildness that flooded her being, the strength, and power. Oh, the power. She could feel it flowing through her body as the phasing sickness began to subside. The aches and pains began to disappear quickly to be replaced with power and strength.

She was finally free from her cage, she thought as the wolf. Standing, she took off running, leaping fully over the body of water to the other side. She landed with the grace only the wolf possessed. This was Remus's territory, but he had given her permission to roam it. She hadn't taken him up on the offer before. The dirt felt good against her paws as she stretched. Then she took off running at an inhuman speed.

Cait was big for a female wolf but was smaller than Remus in his wolf form. She had seen his before, but she was definitely the fastest. Cait had never met a wolf faster than her, and she preferred speed over muscles. It didn't make her any weaker. Her wolf had more powers than the average werewolf. She paused to sniff the air and shook out her white fur. When she phased her eyes changed from their usual blue to match the wolf's inhuman gold. She was no longer just Cait. She was both. Woman and beast united.

Suddenly, several howls rang out in the distance. It seemed Remus had forgotten his offer. His clan had sensed her phasing and were coming to check her out. She decided to meet them first before they could gather in one spot. Cait released her own warning howl. It was a rich and deep song. It dominated the other wolves letting them know a new alpha was on their land. These puppies were no match for her. She was going to show them she was top dog.

Cait had reached the wolves of Remus's clan before they had all gathered. She entered the clearing where the puppies were growling to each other in confusion. They immediately turned their growls on her. She wouldn't be able to hear their inter-clan chatter. That came from the clan bond. So, she waited until they spoke to her. It took a few minutes but eventually, a russet wolf acknowledged her. She could hear the underlying fear in his voice even though he tried to hide it.

"Who are you and what are you doing on our land?" his deep baritone demanded with authority he didn't have.

Cait didn't answer and instead simply stared them down. The wolves quickly became antsy and began to growl at her again.

"Speak wolf!"

"You have no command over me," she replied with power in her voice.

The wolves gave a collective whimper as she commanded the subjugation on them all at once, forcing them to bow their heads. She released it when she felt she had made her point. Immediately, several wolves ran with their tails between their legs. The russet wolf was no alpha and didn't have the command to keep them in order. Even his tail had fallen between his legs as he let out a whimper. The wolves remaining were either frozen in fear or closer to the top of the clan. Cait could smell the stink of fear leaking from them.

"Remus has granted me freedom to these lands."

"Who are you?" the wolf dared to ask.

Cait let out a howl causing the wolves to bark in answer to her calling. They joined her in song.

"I sing the song of Cait Fallon. The last of the Fallon line. I sing the sad tale of the survivor of the massacre. If you know this tale, I bid you to join in this sad song. Let the pain of the Fallon line be known to all who hear it. Let their tale be passed down and let them know that the only survivor lives and is strong. Let them know she is the only white wolf to come from the Fallon's clan. A clan of black wolves. Let it be known she lived without heart. She brought death to her own line. Let it be known that Cait Fallon is the last survivor because she was the executioner. If you hear this sad song, answer its call. Let the pain of the Fallon's be known to all clans. Oh, the great Fallon's. Oh, the strong and powerful Fallon's. Oh, the one without heart."

When Cait finished her song, the wolves in front of her had transformed back into men and all had tears in their eyes. In the distance, pained howls answered the calling. The true song of the Fallon's story. The truth that had been whispered amongst those who were old enough to remember it but didn't dare slander the only survivor. Cait felt her heart ache at the answering howls, but she also felt a sense of relief. Relief that her secret was finally known. She hoped that maybe she could finally begin to heal now that the heavy truth she had always carried with her was out. There would be no more stories of the heroic survivor. There would only be tales that echoed the pain she had felt that night. She would no longer be known as the survivor but as the murderer that she was. It really was a relief. Cait leveled each remaining wolf with her golden gaze. Fallon's had all been black wolves with blue eyes.

The day she had phased into a white wolf with golden eyes was the day she brought shame to her clan. They called her a wolf without heart. They said she was cold and dangerous. She was Cait Fallon. She was Cait Fallon. She was just, Cait Fallon

SNOW'S EYES were red and puffy when she answered the knocking at her front door on Sunday morning. Gwen was standing there looking as haggard as Snow felt. The omega was holding two coffees, one in each hand.

"So you heard it?"

"Heard what?" Snow asked.

Gwen slipped past the brunette, walked down the hall and into the living room. She settled down on the loveseat and patted the spot next to her. Snow closed the door and joined her. Gwen handed her one of the coffee's and let out a long sigh.

"Is she here?"

Snow frowned. "Cait?"

"Who else?"

"No, she left Saturday and hasn't come back."

"She told you her tale then?"

Snow shook her head. "I don't know what you're talking about."

"Why do you look like you've been crying and haven't slept a wink?"

"I don't know. My heart just feels so heavy. Well, I kind of know. After you had left yesterday, Cait and me kind of had a moment."

"A fight?"

"Um, not exactly."

"Jeez, you guys really like to play with fire don't you?" Gwen sighed again.

"I don't think we can help it. It's like I'm just magnetized to her. I don't know; it's just so strong, and I can never think straight."

"Believe me, I understand, I'm just really worried about how strong it became so fast. It really is dangerous, but I get that you can't help it. So what happened? Did someone knock on the door and interrupt you or did you stop her?"

"Neither. She stopped by herself."

Gwen looked honestly surprised. "Really?"

Snow blushed. "Yeah, she just suddenly froze and let out like a whimper or something then poof she was gone."

"Gone?"

"I only heard the front door slam shut."

"Oh, wow. I'll tell you right now that whimper had been one of severe pain. It took a lot of control on her part to leave in the middle of, well, you know what."

Snow nodded.

"And she hasn't been back since yesterday?"

"No. I've tried calling her but she won't pick up."

"Does she feel close?"

"Yeah."

"Then I wouldn't worry."

"Wait, why do you look like you haven't slept?" Snow wondered.

"Well, I just spent twelve hours in labor with a volatile werewolf papa and a momma that nearly squeezed my hand right off my arm. I'm glad to say she is the proud mother of two beautiful baby boys. And then there was the song. We all heard it about an hour before the woman went into labor. I dare say the shock from the song induced pregnancy."

"A song?"

"Do you know of werewolves songs?"

Snow shook her head.

"I'm not surprised." Gwen paused to drink some of her coffee. "We like to keep some clans secrets. Werewolves are taught at a young age how to howl a song. It is the way we pass our stories down from generation to generation. It's a tradition for a pup that reaches their teens to give a song of their triumphs during their first hunt. It's a rite of passage really." Gwen's features darkened. "But the song we heard yesterday was not one of triumph. It was the saddest most shocking song I have ever heard."

"What was it."

Gwen hesitated before she made her decision to answer. "It was Cait's song. The song of the massacre of her clan. The truth of what happened that night."

"Her clan was killed? So the stories my grandmother told me were true then?"

"What exactly did your grandmother tell you?"

"I was very young when I heard my first story about Cait about how she came to know my grandmother. But the first story was the saddest. You have to remember she told it to me in a way that a ten-year-old could partially understand. But I think I understand it more now. I was told that Cait was tricked into giving her wolf over to a bad man and he used her wolf to kill her entire clan."

"What man?" Gwen asked shocked at that little tidbit.

"Don't you know? Didn't you say you just heard Cait's song?"

"There wasn't anything about a man. That's the problem with a song. It's told from the point of view of the singer. Cait was the one that sang it, and it's how she interpreted what happened. I'm interested in Lidia's interpretation. She was a third party to the whole thing. She doesn't carry Cait's guilt which might have skewed her tale a bit. Lidia's would be more objective."

Snow nodded. "I don't know who the man was. My grandmother never told me."

"Can you tell me the story? I'd like to hear it."

"Like I said, it was told to me in a way my ten-year-old brain could understand."

"I don't mind."

"Okay. Grandma told me that Cait had been born without heart. I still don't know what that means. So, she went in search of heart, and she met a bad man. This man promised Cait that he could give her what she was seeking, but she had to promise to relinquish her wolf to him for a whole day. I take it that meant from sun up to sundown. Cait agreed. But the man tricked her, took her wolf and used it to kill her whole clan. When she got it back, she was sad, especially when the man didn't give her what she was seeking. That's when my grandma found her and took her under her wing. And that's basically it."

Gwen mulled this over. "Some of that doesn't make sense to me."

"A lot of it doesn't make sense to me at all." Snow frowned.

"How can someone take control over a werewolf's wolf. That story made it sound like the man separated the two of them. I didn't think that was possible. And what does that bit about heart mean? Cait had said that in her song as well. She spoke of how she was born without heart and that she was the only white wolf born to a clan made up completely of black wolves."

"I don't know. My grandma never explained that bit. She just told me that one day a child would be born that

Cait was supposed to protect and that child would help Cait find her heart."

Gwen looked to Snow in shock. "A child?"

Snow nodded. "I don't know who this child is, but if we can help Cait find it, then we might be able to help her."

Gwen suddenly let out a loud laugh. Snow frowned.

"Why are you laughing? I'm serious. I'm worried about her."

Gwen settled down. "I don't think either of us needs to worry. I have a feeling everything is happening the way Lidia predicted."

"What do you mean? What about the child?"

Gwen smiled. "What child do you know of that Cait promised to protect? The same child that showed up at her homeroom one day and turned her life upside down?"

Snow frowned, opening and closing her mouth several times. No. It wasn't possible. Is that why she had been told all those stories of Cait while growing up? "But..." she trailed off.

Gwen took a swig from her coffee before standing back up and gently patting Snow on the shoulder. "Like I said, everything will work out."

"I need to go home," Snow suddenly blurted out.

"What?"

"I need to go home. I need to speak with my mom, and I miss my parents. Before I moved here, I had a fight with them and had moved into a hotel for a month. I haven't seen them or spoken to them in over a month, but I feel like I need them. I just miss them."

"Whoa, slow down motor mouth. I understand. You want to see your mom. But do you think that's such a good idea right now? Leaving Cait here?"

"You just said everything would be fine."

"I did. Where do your parents live? Can I drive you there? I'd feel safer that way."

"Would you mind? I don't have a car yet."

Gwen grinned. "It would be my pleasure. When do you want to leave?"

"Right now."

"Oh. Okay. How far is it?"

"It's only the next town over. About a two hours drive from here. They allowed me to move out. I never said I moved very far."

## CHAPTER
# ELEVEN

With Gwen's driving, they reached Snow's parent's house in an hour. The werewolf had to peel the brunette out of the car, as she was frozen stiff from all the almost crashes, and hundred miles-per-hour constant speed.

"Come on; my driving isn't that bad. We got here in one piece didn't we."

"I"m driving back."

Gwen chuckled as they walked up the stairs towards the butler waiting at the front door.

"Welcome home, Mistress," came his stiff response.

Snow smiled at him and led Gwen into the main hall.

"Mistress," Gwen teased.

Snow blushed. They entered the main hall where her mother greeted her.

"And the rebellious daughter returns. With a woman no less. Naughty, naughty." Integra wagged her finger as a sensuous smile spread across her lips. Her strawberry blonde hair was pulled up into a messy bun, and her dark eyes were kind but mischievous. When she reached Snow, she pulled her into a warm hug and gave the girl a kiss on the cheek. As they separated, she looked thoughtfully at Gwen. "But not your woman I see. A friend then. It's a pleasure to meet my daughter's first friend. She never brings them here. I dare say she is ashamed of her dear parents."

"Mom!" Snow whined. "You're embarrassing me."

Gwen smiled and shook Integra's hand. She had heard the daughter of Lidia was a salamander that married a human. Gwen had never met a salamander. They were a rare breed. Lidia's husband had been a salamander as well. The werewolf idly wondered if Integra could breathe fire.

"It's a pleasure," Gwen said.

"Believe me; the pleasure is all ours," a male's voice cut in as a dark haired man came down the hall. He swooped down to scoop his daughter into a hug before turning to greet Gwen. "Hello. I'm Adam. Snow's proud father."

Gwen giggled and shook his hand. Adam turned to his wife. "What did I miss?"

"Nothing dear. I was just embarrassing our daughter a little bit. It seems there is indeed a woman."

Adam glanced to Gwen who shook her head. "It's not me."

"You guys! Stop it already. You've embarrassed me enough. I'm sorry I left the way I did. So can you stop teasing me?"

Adam chuckled. "Sorry, dear. It's just too much fun. But maybe we should move this into a more comfortable place. How about the study?"

"Marvelous idea darling. Lead the way," Integra said.

They had to walk down a few halls, and by the time they reached the study Gwen was completely turned around, the only way she could find her way back to the front door would be through scent.

Gwen settled into the seat next to Snow and the girl's parents settled on a loveseat across from them. Snow's parents had an air of nobility about them, but they had a laid back demeanor as if they were able to be flexible to any situation. Integra began.

"So, what brings you home on such short notice. I wasn't expecting you back until the end of the year after the fight we had. I was sure we had finally chased you off for good. "

Adam chuckled. "You make it sound like we wanted her gone."

"Didn't we?" Integra asked coyly.

"I said I was sorry!"

"I'm sorry dear. I couldn't resist. What brings you home?"

Snow glanced over to Gwen silently asking for help, but the werewolf wasn't sure what exactly the girl had wanted to ask her parents. Sadly, mind-reading wasn't one of her powers. She could only shrug in response. Snow looked back to her parents, and Integra decided to try and help her daughter. "Is this about your woman?"

Snow immediately flushed with embarrassment.

"How do you know there's a woman?" her father asked, not puzzled in the slightest. He simply wanted to tease his daughter.

"By the smell of course. A strange smell though it is. I dare say it is familiar though I can't place it."

Gwen took that as her cue. "I can help with that."

All eyes turned to her and while two were questioning one was desperately trying to tell her to stop. Majority won. "Have you ever met Cait Fallon."

Both Adam and Integra shared a look that Gwen couldn't interpret before Adam answered, "We are acquainted with her through Lidia. Though we don't know her very well."

Integra gazed knowingly at her daughter. "Is this Cait person your woman dear?"

"Quit saying it like that."

"Oh, I'm just kidding Snow. Relax, I know you haven't gone past second base as kids say these days."

Gwen watched as Snow's entire body seemed to turn bright red. She was beginning to feel bad for the girl. "Well, we have some questions pertaining to her relationship with Lidia."

"Oh, what kind of questions?"

Gwen had a feeling she was being led astray. There was no way they didn't know who Cait was. She was too famous for people as important as the Bennett's not to know well, especially, since she had been Lidia's personal guard at one point, according to the women herself.

"It's more a question about a story that grandma told me when I was little," Snow finally regained her normal color and found her voice.

"Oh dear, you know those were just fairy tales. Nothing more."

"No, they weren't!" Snow said stubbornly catching her parents off guard with the conviction behind her words.

"Well then, what particular story do you want to know about. I'm afraid I only know a few." Adam placated.

Snow took a deep breath before asking, "I want to know the truth behind how grandma met Cait."

"Well now, that is a story indeed." Integra sighed.

Adam looked startled. "Integra we really shouldn't—"

She cut him off, "Honey, we haven't tricked either of them in the slightest. Believe me; I can smell their conviction from over here. It really was silly for us to think we could keep her in the dark. I thought you were young enough that you would have forgotten all those stories by now. Lidia always did have her own way of doing things. Once I found out exactly the kind of stories she was telling you, I forbid her to continue on the threat that I would keep you from her. But by then the damage had been done." Integra sighed.

Gwen cut in. "Can you explain from the beginning, Mrs. Bennett?"

"Please, call me Integra. You are my daughter's friend. You have earned that right. From the beginning, you ask? Well now, that was a long time ago. I dare say three centuries maybe closer to four. You tend to lose count. Let's just say that it really began after the Treaty of Absolute Peace was signed. I'm sure you know the one I'm speaking of. It's the one that put the Bennett name down in the history books. I was but a simple teenager back then. Young and naive but I was able to pick up on all the whispers going around. The most fascinating one was about the prophecy from the Great Book."

Snow shuddered as she remembered the words of the boy vampire, the dark blood that had cornered her in the hallway. "I know of it."

That surprised Integra. "Mother didn't tell you about that. I'm sure of that. She was the one that created the Silence over that matter. How do you know of it?"

Snow shrunk under their gazes. " I don't want to talk about it."

"Was it from the dark blood that you met at your school?"

Adam jumped up from his seat. "They made contact with you? So soon?"

Even Integra looked shaken. “Well, that changes things.”

“I thought we had another decade,” Adam mumbled sitting back down.

Gwen cleared her throat. “What is the Great Book.”

Integra frowned. “I’m not surprised you don’t know of it. Only a few do. The ones that do are old enough to remember it’s creation or are dark bloods, as it is their book of prophecy.”

“What was the rumor you heard so long ago?” Gwen urged.

“Ah yes, the rumor. I only know what I heard down the chain, but it spoke of a child as cold as ice and her protector. When the Treaty of Absolute Peace was signed not all parties were for it. The dark bloods in particular. The other monsters had forged their signature after their repeated refusal to sign. You have to understand; we were all desperate for peace at that point. The world was at war for a century, and all sides had received heavy casualties. It wasn’t until Lidia came along, with her power of persuasion and ability to control ice, that we were able to bring about a stalemate between all the monster species and the humans. The treaty itself took over a decade to write, and during that time it was a fragile peace. The only monster species that actually thrived during the war were the dark bloods. Disgusting creatures they all are. I assume you don’t know how they are created?”

Gwen and Snow shook their heads.

“Dark bloods are created by draining the blood of a tortured victim. When I say tortured, I mean tortured to the point of insanity. It didn't matter what they were before, monster or human, either would do. So long as they are tortured and drained, they would become one of them.

Both sides, humans, and monsters were equally disgusted by the dark bloods and the treaty was obviously stacked against them, as Lidia hated them. She united the humans and the monsters through their mutual hate and desperate need for peace. The dark bloods didn't take this too well and in a desperate attempt to gain the upper hand killed and turned a famous seer, then forced her to create the Great Book. Thus the prophecy was foretold."

"And that was?" Gwen asked. She was sitting on the edge of her seat.

"I don't know."

"What? Why not?"

"The Silence was enacted shortly afterward by my mother."

"Why?" Snow asked.

"My mother didn't believe that the future was a concrete thing. She firmly believed that people decided their own destiny, so she enacted the Silence to hide the prophecy from the future generations, to give hope and to give us all a fighting chance. Those were her words when I confronted her about it. All I was able to uncover was the bit about the child as cold as ice and her protector. When Snow was born, we were filled with dread, and I turned to my mother. Lidia had simply smiled and called a woman to our house to meet Snow. We didn't understand at first but then she began to tell you stories about the woman. The werewolf named Cait Fallon. The cursed one. You can understand we were furious to have a murderer such as her come near our daughter, not to mention, false stories of her heroics being told to you, Snow."

"Cait isn't a murderer! She's a good person."

Integra sighed. "I know that now. My mother explained

it to me. The truth. I take it that was the story she told you?"

"Yes, but it was the child version. I want to know the adult one."

Integra looked at her husband. "It is in the past, but if it is so important to you, we will tell you."

"Please mother. I need to know."

"Then I shall tell it. You have to understand that we had always known of Cait, but from her day of birth, she was known as the cursed one. The only white wolf among a clan of black. That wasn't the only thing we heard. There was also the rumor of her lacking a heart. At first, we believed this to mean the literal sense but were soon corrected."

"What does it mean?" Snow all but demanded.

"It meant, she was born without a soul," Adam answered.

Snow gasped. "What?"

"It was said, that at birth her soul had been stolen by a goblin and eaten. This is what turned her wolf's coat white. It was also what lead to the great tragedy of her clan. According to my mother, who watched Cait very closely from the time of her birth, the girl was an outcast among her whole clan. People would whisper as she walked by and children shunned her as their noses could detect the lack of a soul in her. Their wolves couldn't trust her, so the humans shunned her. It was even spoken for a time that they should kill her before she reached maturity."

"No!" Snow gasped.

"Her father would have none of that talk either. He and his wife were the only ones to believe their daughter was meant for greatness. Her father was a great alpha and commanded much respect. He alone kept her from the fangs of their clan. But that didn't stop the sadness and emptiness that came from lacking a soul.

My mother recounted the day to me in vivid detail. Cait was the strongest wolf to exist, second only to her father and only because she hadn't fully matured. This caused a lot of fear among the clan and if forced Cait to need to prove herself. My mother said she was ferocious on the battlefield during different clan fights over land. No mercy was shown to her enemies. I guess she had reached a point that she believed if she couldn't gain their love then she would command their fear. But that all changed when a rumor reached her of a man that might be able to help her get back her heart."

"Who was it?" Snow whispered.

"None other than the king of the dark bloods, Xavier."

"Wha...no..why would she..." Snow stumbled over what she wanted to say and just gave up.

"I don't know why she believed a man like him would help her. Some believed he was the one responsible for taking her soul in the first place, but I can only imagine how desperate she was to find a cure for her condition. So, she went to him and pleaded for him to help her. Not much is known of the full powers of the dark bloods. They have managed to keep it a secret, but it is believed they are very powerful. He promised her the cure if she gave him her wolf for one day. From dawn to dawn."

"What did he mean by that? How could she give him her wolf?" Gwen asked.

"As I said, not much is known about the dark bloods, but my mother believed that Xavier has the ability well, more like the magic, to take what is freely offered. He can take the thing people treasure the most. This allows him to grant one wish. The thing is that desperate people never really know what it is they truly treasure. Cait agreed to his conditions, and he took her wolf, using it as the tool to take what she truly held dear. Her clan. Despite the way, they treated her she valued them above everything. So he took her wolf from her body, leaving her in a weakened state, and he used the beast to massacre everyone she ever loved."

"How old was she?" Snow whispered.

"My mother said it happened shortly after her sixteenth birthday. When Cait managed to make it to her home she fought with her clan to stop her wolf, but she was too weak, and all her kinsmen fell one by one until only she was left to face off against the beast. Something happened during that last battle between just her and her wolf. According to my mother, Cait's wolf was supposed to kill her. That was how the promise would have been kept. Her whole clan had to die including her or her wolf, but Cait managed to subdue the beast and reclaim it before dawn, so her end of the bargain to Xavier was unkept, and the deal was off. But the mistake had been made, and the damage was done. That's when my mother Lidia decided to act. She saw that Cait was truly lost and she took the woman under her tutelage. And you know the rest from the stories she told you, Snow."

Snow had tears streaming down her face and wiped at them furiously. Gwen was even dabbing at her own with her sleeve.

"Does that answer your questions, sweetie?" Adam asked softly.

Snow nodded. "Yeah. It does." She hiccuped.

Integra cleared her throat. "Snow, I would like for you to consider staying here. Until we get this whole prophecy thing straightened out. I'm concerned that a dark blood has made contact with you. Whether you are the one they believe you to be or not, dark bloods are dangerous, and it would put my mind at ease to have you close, where we can protect you."

Snow rubbed her eyes dry and shook her head. "No, I'm going back to my apartment tonight. I refuse to put my life on hold because of what some silly book said. I'm going to keep going to school like I planned and finish out my senior year."

Her parents looked ready to argue, but she stood and turned to Gwen. "We're leaving. Right now."

Adam pleaded, "Won't you at least stay for dinner? I'm sure you are tired after the day you've had."

Snow shook her head as Gwen followed her to the door of the study. The brunette didn't even pause as she carelessly tossed an absent goodbye over her shoulder. Her parents continued to follow her all the way to the front door of the mansion.

"Please Snow, stay?" Integra asked.

"I really need to get home. I want to have an early night tonight. I also have tons of homework that I have to catch up on."

"Will you really not stay?" Adam asked as he stopped his daughter once more in the doorway.

"I'm sorry but I really want to be alone right now."

"I know it's a lot to take in Snow, but you don't have to think through it alone. You can do it here in your home."

"My home is two hours away from here as is my bed. I just want to be in my own space. I'm sorry." Snow gave them each a quick hug and a kiss. Her father gripped her tightly and lingered, but she pulled back from him with a small smile.

"I love you guys. Thank you for telling me the truth. I'm glad I know now. It helps."

"You're welcome back anytime honey," Integra said softly.

"I know mom."

"Don't be a stranger. It was nice meeting you Gwen," Adam said.

With one final goodbye, Gwen and Snow climbed into their car, which was right where they left it, parked in front of the mansion's front door. Gwen drove slower back to the apartment. The first hour had been in silence. Each of them processing what they had heard. Finally, Gwen glanced over at her passenger who seemed to be struggling to keep still and broke the silence. "Why did you leave in such a hurry. I'm sure it wouldn't have hurt to have stayed for dinner."

Snow chuckled. "They would have drugged our food. I guarantee it."

Gwen frowned. "They seemed nice."

"Believe me, they are but they were really spooked when they learned that dark blood had spoken to me. You might not have been able to tell, but I know my parents, and I feel like that tidbit of information made them second guess the validity of the prophecy they had probably always thought was just a story. Their reactions are subtle and hard to notice but they are really protective of me. They probably sent one of the bodyguards to follow us home."

"What? Really?"

"I wouldn't put it past them. I'll probably be watched for the next few days but not even I'll be able to pick them out of the crowd. Most of the bodyguards I have never met."

"Wow. I didn't peg them for overbearing parents. They seemed pretty laid back to me."

"My grandparents were the same. They wouldn't let me play in the garden without having an armed guard watching me at all times. But if you spoke to them, you always felt like they were the most reasonable people. Let's just say they are good actors and know the art of manipulation well."

Gwen chuckled. "I'll trust you on this one."

Snow smiled and looked out her window.

"So is that the only reason we left in such a hurry?"

"Cait is calling me."

"I didn't hear your cell phone?"

"Not that way. I just feel like she worrying about where I am."

Gwen gasped. "What? You can already feel her?"

Snow nodded. "Sometimes. I just get this feeling. Like when she wants me close or if she's angry."

"Wow. You two really are something. Usually, it takes months before a connection that strong is formed. Especially, if you haven't even bonded yet. You two continue to surprise me with your progress,"

Snow chuckled.

"So, she's calling you home?"

"Not specifically but I can tell she doesn't know where I am. She became aware of it while we were speaking with my parents. I felt her presence shift and become restless. She's been calling to me since."

"Well, we will be back soon. We probably should have told her where we were going before we left."

"I didn't think she would even notice. We were only gone for a few hours. I left my cell phone in my bedroom in my rush to leave."

"Guess it was long enough."

"Guess so."

# CHAPTER TWELVE

Cait was confused. She had shown up at Snow's apartment immediately after feeling the girl's presence getting farther away. She pulled out her cell phone for the hundredth time and saw there were no missed calls. The werewolf felt the insistent urge to call the girl, but she didn't want to come off as clingy or controlling. The redhead knew that if she called Snow now she wouldn't be able to stop herself from demanding where the girl was, why she left, and for her to come back right this instant. In that order. It was scary how her wolf had begun to fuse with her more fully, and she was beginning to find it hard to differentiate between her beast's demands and her human ones. She had felt the girl before she heard the key enter the lock. Before she had a coherent thought, she was throwing the door open in seconds and had pushed past Gwen, to pull Snow into her arms.

"Hey! I'm not some box you can just shove aside. I'm a person!" Gwen huffed as she regained her balance.

"Where did you go, why did you leave without telling

me?" Cait demanded as soon as she pulled back to meet the girl's gaze.

It was an understatement to say she was surprised when Snow suddenly burst into tears, pulled the werewolf back to her and buried her face into her neck. Cait immediately rubbed her back soothingly. "Hey, what's the matter? Are you hurt?"

She glanced at Gwen who shrugged and walked past them into the apartment, going straight into the kitchen to look for food.

"Cait." Snow wailed and gripped the redhead tighter. Cait sighed and scooped the girl into her arms, carrying her into the apartment, and kicking the door shut. She headed towards the bedroom.

"No hanky panky!"

Cait rolled her eyes and shut the bedroom door behind her before laying Snow down on the bed. The girl refused to separate from her and clung to her like a baby Koala. Cait had to awkwardly maneuver herself onto the bed where she then tucked Snow into her side. The girl was practically laying on top of her as every inch of her body was touching the werewolf. The redhead felt her wolf clawing at her mental cage. The need to comfort her mate was overwhelming.

"Snow, what's wrong? What happened today?" she asked softly.

Snow's sobs had begun to slow, and now she only hiccuped occasionally, but she remained glued to the werewolf, clinging to her.

"I went to see my parents today," Snow mumbled against Cait, so the woman felt more then she heard the answer.

"Did they upset you?"

"No."

"Then why are you crying?"

Snow hiccuped and moved back enough to gaze up into the werewolf's electric blue eyes, and she whispered, "You have no heart."

Cait tensed as the haunting words that had followed her throughout her lifetime were repeated with such sadness by her mate.

"Where did you hear that phrase?" she whispered, and her blood turned cold.

"From my mother."

Cait sighed. The salamander must have heard it from Lidia. It was only a matter of time before her mate came to learn of it as well.

"I see." Cait tried to retreat but Snow buried her face back into her neck and gripped her more tightly.

"Don't Cait."

The werewolf sighed again and tightened her hold on her mate. "I take it she told you the story then from your reaction?"

Snow nodded. Her lips brushing lightly against the werewolf's neck making her shiver. "If she heard it from Lidia then she probably knows quite a bit of the story. What did she tell you?"

"That it wasn't your fault."

Cait felt her whole body sag as she released a breath. Lidia had been too kind, but at the same time, the one person she didn't want to think of her as the murderer that she was, was Snow. She wanted the girl to trust her. How could someone like the girl in her arms, trust a woman that killed her entire family.

"I killed them all Snow. Every last one of them. It was all my fault."

"No, it wasn't!" the girl responded petulantly. She was as stubborn as her grandmother. Cait didn't know whether to be amused or grateful. She was a little bit of both.

"Then whose fault was it?"

"Xavier's."

A loud guttural growl ripped from Cait's throat before she could stop it.

"It was all his fault, Cait. None of it was yours."

Cait sighed. "You're as kind as your grandmother, Snow. And though I agree Xavier holds some of the blame, it was my wolf he used to kill them."

"But you fought with them, to protect them."

"A lot of good that did anyone."

Snow paused then asked the question she had been wondering since she heard the story from her mother. "How did you stop your wolf from killing you?"

"What?"

"My mother said Lidia had told her that after everyone was dead that you faced off against your wolf. She said that Xavier had planned for one of you two to die. How did you get back control of it before dawn came?"

"You are well informed. Well, I should say that Lidia had a big mouth and a need to pass along stories to the next generation."

"She always loved story time with me."

Cait smiled softly. "It's kind of hard to explain what happened before dawn on that day."

"Try me."

The woman sighed and adjusted herself into a more comfortable position. She cleared her throat and began.

THEY WERE ALL DEAD. Cait gazed around her to her fallen kinsmen. Their broken and bloody bodies littered the ground like fallen soldiers. She couldn't even save one of them. She felt anger and sadness fill her, fuel her, as she stared down the white beast that committed the crime. Her wolf. The once golden eyes were blood red with the spell Xavier had cast on it. The wolf bared its fangs at her.

"You don't scare me!" the sixteen-year-old yelled back even as her legs wobbled unsteadily. Her wolf had always been powerful. Too powerful. She was never able to fully control it when she went out onto the battlefield. Its thirst for blood knew no bounds, and it usually took all her willpower to prevent it from turning on her own people during a fight. She had finally failed. The beast was out of control and its old and ancient power tinged the air with electricity. How could she defeat something so much stronger than her? Even her father, the strongest wolf she had ever known had succumbed to the beast's teeth. How was she, reduced to a mere human for a day, supposed to kill a werewolf? She glanced down at her claymore. It was a blade of the Fallon Clan, crafted from the finest metals. When she and her beast were one, she had the strength the lift the heavy blade. Now it hung limply at her side as her arms struggled with its immense weight.

The white wolf growled as if laughing at her weakness.

"Shut up!" she yelled before charging the wolf, dragging the blade along the ground as she ran with speed fueled by anger and loss.

The wolf charged as well. They met in the middle of the battlefield with metal against fang. Cait had found the strength at the last minute to swing the claymore up to meet the wolf's teeth, and the blade sparked with flames. They pushed against their own respective weapons. Each was trying to gain the upper hand. Something registered in the back of Cait's mind causing her to lose her focus a minute and allowing the wolf to gain the upper hand. She began to lose ground. Something was wrong, she thought, as she dug her feet deep to prevent the wolf from pushing her back. What was that feeling? It had cut through her own anger and sorrow. She concentrated on it, and suddenly it was as if she released the floodgates. The feeling of overwhelming pain and sadness knocked the breath from her lungs causing her to fall back. The wolf was towering over her now as she lay on her back holding the blade like the final barrier it was between life and death.

Where was that pain coming from? It didn't feel like hers. She tried to brush it off. To push it back so she could concentrate on the battle but it demanded her attention. It consumed her. She cried out from the depths of the pain that was filling her being. Where was it coming from? Her electric blue eyes met that of the wolf's blood red, and she saw into the mind of the beast attempting the devour her. She saw the wolf behind Xavier's control. She saw herself.

"You?" she cried out as the teeth were nearly at her throat.

"Why?" she yelled.

And the wolf answered without words. The feelings flooded into her, and she translated their meaning. "What have you made me do?"

"I'm sorry!" she cried out and thrust the blade up but only managed to push the teeth an inch back.

"I have killed them all. My family. Why did you make me do this?" it asked.

"I was in so much pain." Cait cried out.

"We would have endured. Can we endure this?"

"I don't know."

"Why have you betrayed me?"

"Betrayed?"

"You gave me to another."

"I'm sorry! I was stupid. I didn't think."

"I should kill you. Eat you like the rest."

"No! I refuse to give up. I want my revenge."

"Revenge?"

"Against Xavier. I want his blood on my blade."

"Yes! We want his blood."

"I need your power! I need your strength. I am weak alone."

"I need your mind and your body." the wolf agreed.

"Come back to me then! And we will hunt the man that betrayed us."

The wolf was silent for a moment before it slowly began to move back away from her. Its eyes were still blood red, and it still bared its fangs, but it was no longer at her throat.

"We must make a new oath. The spell must be broken, and there is not much time."

"I will sing a new oath." Cait panted.

The wolf lifted its mighty muzzle into the sky and let loose a beautiful song, "I sing the song of the cursed one. Let all who are near answer my call. I sing an oath stronger than blood. Let it be known that today is the day the cursed one slew her clan. Let it be known that she betrayed her wolf. I sing of a promise made among the bodies of her people on the battlefield. Let her promise be heard."

The wolf paused to look at Cait who drew a deep breath before answering the song. Her voice was rough from screaming during the fight, but it was heavy with emotion, and determination. "I sing the song of the one without heart. Let all who are near answer my call. Let it be known that the wolf listened to the plea of a murderer. Let it be known that she was weak and pitiful. I sing of an oath stronger than blood. Let me speak my piece. I swear to never betray my wolf again. I swear never to succumb to our sorrows. Not until we kill the man who betrayed us. I swear to live my days until I claim Xavier's blood with our fangs. I swear to carry on the Fallon Clan's legacy. Let my oath be known on this battlefield among the body of my kinsmen. Let it be known to the wolf I have betrayed," Cait sang with everything she was and when she stopped her wolf answered in a haunting sound filled with finality.

It howled, "The oath has been accepted. To fail this promise, that surpassed blood will be the end of us both. I swear to my master once more my servitude in her life. The oath has been made it shall never be forgotten," the howl ceased, and Cait felt ancient power tinge the air with the smell of smoke before she met the wolf's gaze once more. Golden eyes welcomed her, and she moved to touch it. To feel its power once more. At her touch, the wolf disappeared in a blinding white light, and Cait felt its presence within her body and mind once more.

The whispered promise, "Do not forget."

Cait looked up as the first rays of sunlight flooded the sky. The night had taken with it the souls of the fallen. The lone survivor stood and let the light burn away her mistakes. She could only move forward. She would. As her song promised.

# CHAPTER THIRTEEN

Several tears trailed down Snow's cheeks, and Cait kissed them away. "Don't cry, Snow. It was a long time ago."

"Oh, Cait. I'm so very sorry." Snow hugged the werewolf closer to her.

"Shh, it's okay."

They rocked back and forth until the girl gained control over the sobs that were wracking her body and stilled against the werewolf.

"Cait?" came her small whisper.

"What is it, baby?"

Snow liked it when the woman called her that. "Let's do the blood bond thing."

Cait tensed as her wolf made itself known in the form of her body heating up. She pushed it down and gritted her teeth taking a deep breath. The girl in her arms seemed to have felt the burst of heat and responded in kind. Snow had begun to nibble on Cait's neck as her hand clumsily slipped under Cait's t-shirt. The werewolf grabbed the traveling hand and intertwined their fingers before softly drawing Snow's head back.

"No, Snow."

This seemed to make Snow tremble, and Cait quickly recognized the flash of hurt at her perceived rejection. The girl tried to pull away, but Cait held her fast and made her meet her gaze. "Snow. It's not what you think. I want to go through the blood bond with you. Believe me, I ache to complete it and finally have you as mine."

Snow saw a little bit of gold trickle into the werewolf's eyes at her declaration, and Snow knew she was answering as both the wolf and the woman. "But I want to do it when you're ready to accept me. And not out of pity."

"It's not pity!"

"Then why?"

"I care about you, Cait. I want you to finally be happy after everything you've gone through!"

Cait sighed. "Your intentions may be pure but they a very innocent. The blood bond is permanent Snow. You would be stuck with me for the rest of your life. It affects you as much as it affects me. It's not just something we do then we go our separate ways and live out our lives. It is a ritual in which we swear our devotion to one another. Have you even decided how you want me to fit into your life?"

"I know I want you in it."

"But how? Would you remain my friend or would you be willing to devote your body, mind, and soul completely to me as I would to you, and become my lover?"

Snow blushed and looked down at their joined hands. They fit perfectly together. "No, I don't know yet. But I want you always to be close by...I know I don't like you disappearing for too long. I missed you when you left me so suddenly on Saturday, Cait. I had felt like something was missing as I waited for you to come back. I could still feel you close by, but I want to see you every day. I want to hold your hand like this every day. What I'm trying to say is that I'm not sure about a lot of things, but one thing I know is that you're an irreplaceable part of my life and if you were ever to leave me it might kill me."

Cait brought their joined hands to her mouth and kissed her knuckles. "I'll never leave you, Snow. That I promise you."

Snow smiled and began to say something but suddenly broke into a yawn.

"That's enough talking for today. We have school tomorrow, and you need your rest." Cait chuckled and began to climb off the bed.

"Stay," the word left Snow's mouth before she could stop herself.

Cait stopped. "I don't know..."

"I want you to stay." Snow gripped her shirt.

"I don't know if I'm strong enough."

The girl pulled her closer. "You are. I trust you, Cait."

The werewolf filled with warmth at her mate's words and settled back on the bed. "Until you fall asleep then."

"The whole night," Snow demanded, and Cait chuckled.

"We'll see."

"Cait--"

"I said we'll see. Go to sleep now. I can see you drooping with exhaustion."

Snow yawned again and pulled the covers up higher and settled against the warmth of the woman next to her. She relaxed as the feeling of safety and the smell of rain-water surrounded her. She sighed as she felt deft fingers threading through her hair softly in a soothing motion.

Snow didn't know when exactly she fell asleep, but it was to the strong beat of her werewolf's heart.

AIDEN GREY WAS a dark blood and not just any dark blood. He was the youngest to have been knighted in their long history. Men and women bowed their heads in respect as he passed them in the hallway on his way to the throne room. They all stank of fear as he brushed past them. Aiden grinned. His reputation preceded him, and this made him happy. He didn't need friends, only soldiers, servants, and slaves. The only favor he cared to nurture was that between him, and the king, and the queen. They were all that mattered. They understood his ways, and it always entertained them when he told them of his latest victims. Aiden paused in front of the doors that led to the throne room and glared at the servant shaking in front of him.

"Announce me," he demanded.

The man moved quickly and burst through the doors before calling out, "Sir Aiden of the house of Grey." The servant moved aside, and Aiden pushed him when he didn't move fast enough. The boy made a beeline for the throne and kneeled at the foot of his leaders.

"Rise Sir Aiden," came a deep baritone that caused a shiver to run down the boy's spine. He stood and met the cold red eyes of the king. "King Xavier. I have come at your request."

Aiden heard a quiet giggle to his left and glanced over to see Queen Xena, hiding her face behind a paper fan. The king's voice commanded his attention back.

"It has come to my notice that you have made contact with the ice child."

Aiden paused before nodding his head.

"I thought I commanded you to stay from their notice?"

"I don't understand why you need concern yourself with those weaklings your highness. They are but mere insects to your great power."

"You do not need to know. I gave you orders, and you failed in them."

"I could have killed the ice child. She is so weak. Her protector is no match for my power either. Let me kill them for you and put an end to this stupid prophecy!" Suddenly, pain exploded in his skull, and Aiden screamed, dropping to the ground and spasming on the floor. The pain was unbearable, and it was gone as quickly as it came. The knight lay on the floor. Every nerve felt like it was exposed and burned.

"Good knight. You do not question the great king. You do his bidding." The queen giggled snapping her fan closed and showing off her fangs.

"I'm sorry," Aiden said in a hoarse voice.

"Good. Now the king has new orders for you. Take care to listen. We will not tolerate another failure."

Aiden forced himself up so that he kneeled before them again. His body shook with the effort.

"Sir Aiden, I want you to bring the ice child to me."

"Here?"

"Did the great king stutter?"

"No. I will do as you bid. Is there anything else?"

"That will suffice," came Xavier's reply.

Aiden stood but wobbled a little before steadying. He left the throne room with his head held high along with one thought. He would capture the ice child known as Snow Bennett, but he would have fun with her before turning what's left of her over to the king.

When Snow felt her consciousness return, as a new day began, she felt warm all over, and quickly became acutely aware of several things at once, upon opening her eyes. The first was that she was flushed and horny as hell. She could feel her damp panties, as well as the muscular thigh, pressed tightly against her most intimate spot. Next, her notice was drawn to the hot hand palming her naked breast. Somehow, her shirt and bra had been taken off in the middle of the night. She was thankful her shorts were still where she left them. She moaned as hot breath fanned across her beaded neglected nipple and looked down to see Cait's sleeping face resting on her chest. How was she doing this in her sleep?

Snow's breath was shallow, she gasped when Cait shifted, and the thigh between her legs rubbed against her hot center. She couldn't help jerking her hips against the hard thigh and the whimper that left her at the friction it created. She felt Cait's soft lips trail up her collarbone and settle against her neck. She didn't know how to get free, and she wasn't entirely sure she wanted to.

"Cait?"

The woman mumbled but didn't wake.

Snow tried again.

"Cait? Wake up." She tried nudging the werewolf. That roused her.

"Snow?" came her rough reply.

"Hey." Snow smiled at the adorable picture the woman made.

Cait raised her head and smiled sleepily at Snow. "Good morning," she mumbled her voice still heavy with sleep. When she shifted, her thigh rubbed harder against Snow, and the girl's breath hitched. Cait looked at her in confusion. The werewolf moved her hand and felt something soft and supple in her palm. She squeezed and watched Snow gasp and pulled her bottom lip between her teeth. The redhead looked down to her hand and jerked it back as if she'd been burned.

"Shit! I'm so sorry." Cait moved to sit up and felt her thigh slide against something and heat ignited against it. She glanced down again and saw what exactly her leg was rubbing against. She jumped up quickly, and her feet got tangled up in the bedsheets. There was a loud thump followed by a groan of pain. Snow sat up and looked over the edge of her bed to see the werewolf sprawled out on the wooden floor holding her elbow. She couldn't help the giggle that followed the concern.

"Are you okay?"

"I think so," Cait said as she rubbed the quickly forming bruise on her elbow. The skin became a light brown, but a second later it disappeared, and Cait stood.

"You heal quickly."

"Mostly small stuff. Anything deadly takes a lot longer." Cait smiled at the girl but quickly looked away.

"Cait?"

"I'll just let you get dressed," she mumbled, and was out of the bedroom in seconds, closing the door softly behind her. Snow frowned in confusion. What was that about? She sat back on the bed and felt the coldness of her sheets against naked skin. She looked down. Oh, that's why. She thought and blushed. She climbed off the bed and ignoring the wet sticky feeling between her leg, set about getting ready for school.

❄

SNOW COULD FEEL the heat of his gaze burning a hole in the back of her head. She shifted uncomfortably at her desk. The dark blood that had threatened her was still in her homeroom. Honestly, she had hoped he would disappear or something. He scared her. She knew Cait could sense her discomfort as she kept shooting her worried looks as she said some of the morning announcements. Snow gave her a small smile and watched the werewolf relax slightly. The hot gaze was suddenly gone, and she let out a breath. Finally.

"How was your weekend?" Sarah asked.

Snow looked over to the siren and shook her head. "I had to visit my parents."

"Oh, that's right you live by yourself. Did you forget something at home?"

"No, I just wanted to visit them. They don't live very far from me. I spent the weekend unpacking and just missed them."

Sarah smiled. "Well, my weekend was boring with a capital 'B'. I just spent it doing homework and watching TV. My little brother was a real pain. There were many battles waged over the remote most of which I'm proud to say I won." She smirked.

Snow giggled, but it was smothered by the bell ringing.

"See you later, Snow."

She waved as the siren picked up her bag and filed out of the classroom along with the mob of students going to their first class of the day. She sighed and reached into her messenger bag to retrieve her book. She was behind on pages, and her teacher was the one to blame. Snow rubbed the sleep from her eyes. Exhaustion from everything that had happened in the past few days had begun to settle in.

The brunette used to think her life was boring, and to

be honest, it kind of had been. She had a sheltered childhood, and though she loved her parents, they were overbearing and tended to smother her. Snow could remember it had only been a few days ago that she wished for an adventure and a little excitement. Well, that's exactly what she got. Cait was the spice that her life lacked.

The werewolf was talking to a student that had just entered, and it looked like she was scolding him. Her usually wild mane of red locks was pulled back into a high ponytail though a few strands had escaped. Cait had her hands on her hips and was speaking quietly to the boy while he had his head bowed. She shifted from one foot to the other and Snow saw the muscles in her legs ripple in her tight jeans from the movement.

She took in the woman at the front of the classroom in all her dominating glory. Cait was beautiful. The werewolf didn't look a day over twenty. Her muscles weren't large and bulky, but instead, she was toned. Snow could remember the hard warmth of the woman's abs when she had rubbed her core against them to get friction. She felt a blush stain her cheeks, and her body heat up, her core ached. She rubbed her legs together to relieve some of the ache and saw Cait's body tense. The werewolf stopped mid-sentence, and zeroed in on Snow, catching her gaze with her electric blue eyes that flashed gold for a second.

# CHAPTER FOURTEEN

Cait had been telling Takeshi that he needed to remember not to let his wings out in the hallway. She had witnessed the tengu, also known to some as a crow demon, shoot one wing out to push another student into a locker. He was just playing a prank, and she had been warned by the other teachers that he was a troublemaker, but she wanted to give him the benefit of the doubt.

Tengu were noble demons originating from Japan, and though they were taught early on to uphold the honor of their flocks, the younger ones tended to go through a stage of rebellion. Cait had seen it time and time again while teaching. Young tengu were mean and could sense weakness which usually led to them playing pranks.

"Takeshi, promise me you won't do it again or--" Her wolf suddenly slammed against her mental cage and she felt heat explode in her chest cutting her off mid-sentence. Cait's gaze was locked in on her mate instantly.

Snow had her bottom lip between her teeth, and her face was flushed. Cait could feel the girl's need like it was her own. She was calling to her, and Cait's wolf was responding in kind. She took a step forward.

"Ms. Fallon?" She heard her name through the fog and glanced back to the boy. He gasped and took a step back as his eyes widened. She could smell the fear rolling off of him.

"I promise, I won't do it again," he whispered and took off, not stopping until he was safely at his desk.

She closed her eyes and breathed through her nose grinding her teeth. Stay in control, she berated herself. This was at school for christ's sake. If she wasn't careful, she would pounce on the poor girl and take her in the middle of the classroom.

The bell for class to begin rang, cutting off her inner thoughts, and helping to clear her head. She rubbed her eyes, and though the wolf was still prowling back and forth, it had settled. Sighing, she went back over to the podium at the front of the classroom and retrieved the worksheets she had printed off that morning. She walked to the row of students on the far left and counted out enough sheets, before handing them to the student in front. The girl took one and passed the rest to the boy behind her. Cait continued to hand out the sheets and spoke,

"This is a worksheet with questions about the first ten chapters of Frankenstein. I want you to work on them quietly. You can work on them together if you like. We will go over them tomorrow in class." She handed the boy in the last row a stack of papers then made her way to her desk in the back of the classroom. Cait passed Snow on her way back and swallowed hard to keep herself in check. All she had to do was get through school, then she and Snow were going to have a talk, back at the girl's apartment. A long talk.

By the time she got off the bus and walked to her apartment, Snow was feeling even more tired than from the beginning of the day. School had exhausted her more than usual. Before she had left to find her bus, Cait had pulled her aside at the end of homeroom. She blushed at the memory.

"Hey, are you alright?"

Snow nodded, but Cait wasn't convinced. The girl was practically drooping where she stood.

"Yes, just tired. I think I might take a nap when I get home."

Cait smiled softly as the girl gave a huge yawn. "Okay, well I'm going to be late coming over today. I have a few errands I have to run and to get some things from my apartment."

"Oh, okay." Snow paused and frowned at the thought of Cait not being there until later. When had she become so used to the werewolf's presence that she felt a sense of loss when she was missing.

"I won't be long, promise."

"No, it's okay. You have your own life. Actually, you don't have to come over if you have things you need to do." Snow's gut dropped. Why had she said that? Of course, the redhead had to come over. She was supposed to.

Cait frowned. "I'll be back by seven. You won't even notice I'm gone."

"I'll notice," Snow blurted out before she could stop herself.

Cait smirked, a sexy tilt of the lips that drew Snow's gaze to them. "Will you miss me?"

Snow blushed and turned away from the woman's

tempting lips. They looked so firm, but she could feel the ghost memories of their softness against her own, sliding down her neck, drawing her breast into a hot mouth. The werewolf growled lowly in her chest drawing Snow's attention to the woman in front of her. Cait's eyes were shut tightly and her body tense.

"Cait?"

"Just a minute."

The girl made to move closer when she was interrupted by the sound of a girl's nasally voice.

"Ms. Fallon, I had a question about--" Cait grabbed Snow pulling her into her chest, and turned, letting loose a low growl at the girl behind them. The student backtracked.

"Sorry, I'll figure it out myself!" She ran until she was in the hallway. Snow glanced around the room afraid other students were around but released a breath when she saw they were alone.

"Cait, you can let me go now," she said softly.

The werewolf ignored her in favor of nuzzling into her hair. She reached Snow's ear and licked the outer shell drawing a gasp from the girl in her arms.

"Cait we can't. We're at school. Someone might see us."

"No one's here," came the deep-throated response.

"Someone might come in." Snow knew she was fighting a losing battle. Even as she gave reasons to stop, her traitorous hands were pulling at Cait's t-shirt drawing her closer. The redhead's nose brushed against her own and their lips slid against each other roughly. Snow could feel the werewolf's need to taste more of her as if it was her own. The brunette couldn't resist peeking her tongue out to slide against Cait's lips. The werewolf gave a throaty moan and picked Snow up by her ass. The girl gasped and wrapped her legs around the werewolf and her arms around her neck. Cait took the moment of shock to take control and dominate the girl's mouth. Her tongue entered unrepentantly and explored until meeting Snow's tongue sliding the silky muscles against each other.

Snow moaned and pulled Cait closer into her, running her finger into red locks, tugging. She needed more of her; she needed to be closer, she needed all of her. "Cait," she groaned when the woman's hand snuck up her shirt trailing lightly against her skin drawing goosebumps. Snow faintly heard the clearing of a throat but was distracted by the tongue dominating her mouth. The girl heard it again though louder this time. She opened her eyes slightly only to see Remus standing in the doorway. She froze, then pulled away from the kiss. Cait moved with her but wasn't fast enough to reclaim her lips and let out a growl.

"What's wrong?" she whispered.

"I don't think this is really appropriate for school Cait," Remus said evenly. "Or safe for that matter."

Cait rolled her eyes and set Snow down. The girl released her hold and let her legs drop down before setting about straightening her school polo. She could feel a deep blush staining her cheeks. Cait fixed her hair, and after checking Snow turned to meet the other werewolf, as well as her boss.

"Remus."

"I came to check on you. I wasn't expecting Ms. Bennett to be here." He frowned.

Cait didn't respond.

"I'm lending you my omega to keep things from getting out of hand, and therefore dangerous. If you're just going to do it here, then you won't be needing Gwen. You'd just be wasting all our time."

Cait fixed a glare on the werewolf in front of her. Had he always been this annoying? She must have just ignored him most of the time. "I still need Gwen. And you're not lending her. She's was never yours to begin with. She belongs to herself."

"She's in my clan!" he growled.

"By her own right!" she yelled back.

Snow stepped between the two wolves and held up her hands. "Mr. Remus. I'd really appreciate it if Gwen could come over again tonight. We still need her help."

Remus sighed. "Just be careful you two. I don't want to see either of you get hurt. Despite what you may think Cait, I like you, and would hate to lose a wolf like yourself."

Cait nodded and stuck her hands into her jean pockets. She was lucky Remus was so laid back about the dress code at the school for the teachers. She didn't know what she would do without pockets. "We will."

"Good. That's all. Ms. Bennett, if you hurry you should still be able to catch your bus."

The girl actually paled. "Yes, sir!" she yelped, ran to her desk, and scooped up her backpack. "See you at home, Cait!" she called out and was out the door in a second flat.

Remus raised an eyebrow. "At home?"

"Oh drop it." the redhead grumbled and walked over to her desk to collect her things.

CAIT PAUSED, took a deep breath, then pushed her way into the boxing club. Two men were in the ring; the red boxer had the upper hand. Cait smiled as she recognized him as one of Nathan's more experienced kickboxers. She gave a sweep of the room but didn't see Nathan anywhere. She turned back in time to see the red kick-boxer deliver a swift kick to the blue boxers head. He won the match. There were cheers from the crowd that surrounded the ring, and the red boxer went to his corner to retrieve his water bottle and towel. Cait met him there.

"I'm looking for Nathan. Do you know where he is?"

"Smoke break out back," he said before taking a swig of water. She nodded and dodged a few sweaty teenagers making her way to the back door. She didn't think Nathan was a smoker. He never smelt like burning tobacco. Her suspicions were confirmed when she opened the back door, and although the area smelt heavily of smoke, Nathan didn't carry the burning smell. He looked up and met her gaze. A small smile broke out across his face.

"You came back."

Cait returned the smile and walked out taking a seat next to him on the bench. She rested her elbows on her thighs and stared in front of her. They sat in silence a moment before Nathan broke it.

"Cait I'm--"

She cut him off, "Sorry, Nathan." She turned to him. He looked surprised.

"I shouldn't have yelled at you like I did. You didn't know better. I never told you my circumstances so I shouldn't have snapped at you like that. You were only trying to help."

"I'm sorry as well. Sometimes my mouth gets away from me. I should have picked up on your subtle hints. I'm kind of an idiot sometimes, and my sister loves to call me thick skulled and dense."

Cait chuckled. "You are that."

Another silence fell between them, but it was comfortable. Nathan sighed and stood. "How about I go a round with you? I need to blow off some steam."

"Something bothering you?"

"Let's just say you aren't the only one with girl problems." Cait laughed.

"Then let's go a few rounds."

"I'll warn you inuyoukai don't like to lose."

Cait stood as well. "Well, get used to it because you're not going to win."

"Big words for such a small woman." He laughed and held the door open for her.

"I'm not small."

"To me you are."

"But, you're a giant! You can't use yourself as a comparison."

"I just did."

"That's it. First shot's going to be to that thick skull of yours."

"I'd like to see you try." He laughed as the door swung shut behind him.

# CHAPTER FIFTEEN

A loud thumping startled Snow awake. At first, she was confused, but she quickly came to her senses and glanced at her alarm clock. It read seven in the evening. She smiled and jumped off the bed. She ran until she reached the door but caught her reflection in the hallway mirror. The brunette paused a moment to run her fingers through her hair and straighten her t-shirt, rubbing out some of the wrinkles. The knocking came again. She rushed to the door and threw it open without checking through the peep hole. The smile on her face contorted into an open scream at the boy standing before her. A cloth covered her nose and mouth; she fought her attacker, but he was too strong as he pulled her out into the hallway. A sharp smell filled her nose, and mouth, as her vision darkened.

"Cait," she slurred as she lost consciousness.

Aiden threw the limp form of the girl over his shoulder. He needed to hurry. Her scream had alerted the curiosity of the neighbors. Quickly, he ran to the stairwell and pushed open the door. He really got her! Excitement bubbled up in his chest. It was so easy. He had thought he would have to take on that fleabag that was always with her, but he was so lucky! She had been alone, and now she was all his. A laugh bubbled up and out his mouth, as he hit the streets, and opened the back door to his black Sedan. He pulled out the rope, tied Snow's hands together behind her back, then settled her into the trunk. The dark blood quickly closed the trunk and settled behind the wheel.

He really did it! He laughed again and started the engine. It was a long drive to where they were going. He had used enough of the drug to hopefully keep her unconscious until then. Aiden pulled out onto the main road and turned on the radio. Classical music filled the Sedan, and he felt the adrenaline subside. He didn't have to rush. She was his until tomorrow afternoon. Only then would he hand her over to his king. Though, they wouldn't recognize her once he's through with her.

Unadulterated fear burst from Cait's chest making her pause mid-swing. Nathan took advantage of her distraction to sucker punch her. She stumbled back but caught herself on the rope. She held up her gloved hand, and Nathan stopped.

"Giving up already?" he panted and wiped a trickle of blood from under his nose.

She shook her head catching her breath. "Something's wrong."

"What?"

"I...I have to go," she said and pulled the ropes apart so she could climb through them.

"Hey, wait up Cait."

"I have to go!" Cait growled and jumped down to the floor. She threw the headgear and gloves at one of the students that had been watching the match. He fumbled with them before getting hold of them. Nathan walked over to the rope.

"Cait!" he called after her. But she was already out the door.

She made it to her car and started the engine. The numbers on the dashboard caught her attention, eight o' clock. She was late, and the feeling of foreboding was like acid in her gut. The connection she had with Snow was faint and told her that the girl was either asleep or unconscious. The redhead hopped the former was true. She needed to get to their apartment, and she needed to get there now. Cait pulled out onto the main road and floored the gas.

CAIT CHARGED out of the elevator and stopped in front of the apartment. The scent she caught as her hand reached for the doorknob, made her blood run cold, and her wolf bang against her mental cage. A dark blood had been there. A snarl ripped from her lips, and the front door flew open revealing Gwen.

"She's gone."

"I'll kill them!" Cait yelled and turned to leave.

"Cait wait!" Gwen grabbed her shoulder spinning the werewolf around. The redhead bared her teeth at her.

"Don't give me that! You can't go running in there fangs and claws bared."

"Why the hell not!"

"You need to calm down and think logically about what we need to do."

"I need to kill them all." A slap rang out in the empty hallway. Cait's head jerked to the side from the force of it. She shook her head to clear it and turned to face Gwen.

"Thanks, I needed that," she mumbled.

"No problem. Now, here's what we need to do. I know you can track Snow down by using your connection. I hear you're also fast as hell in your wolf form. So, this is what we will do. I'm going to call Remus and meet up with him first. We will meet up with you when we can."

"I don't need his help."

"We need backup, Cait. We might be outnumbered with just the two of us."

"Fine, do what you want. I'm going."

Gwen sighed and followed while pulling out her cell phone. She really hoped they could make it in time. Fear gripped in her chest at the thought of either Cait or Snow being hurt. They were like her sisters now, like clan mates, family. Remus's voice on the other end of the line interrupted her thoughts as the elevator opened. Cait charged out to the street and burst into her wolf form. She really was majestic. Truly of strong blood. Gwen could feel the power in the air around Cait. Their eyes met briefly, then the white werewolf took off in the direction of the forest, dodging traffic. Luckily, there wasn't much this time of the day in this area. Only a few people lined the sidewalks, and some were pointing, but it wasn't like werewolves weren't allowed to be in their beast forms in public. Most just preferred the privacy of the forest.

"Gwen? Something wrong?" Remus asked.

She snapped out of her thoughts. She had a job to do.

"Remus, I need your help."

When Snow woke, it was with a foggy mind. Where was she? She wondered as she tried to process what she was seeing. The room was spacious, and the walls were made of logs. A cabin? How did she get here? She tried to raise her hand to her pounding head but wasn't able to move it. She looked down only to realize she was tied to a wooden chair. Both her hands and legs were tied to it, and she tested the bonds. They were holding. Fear sent a shiver down her spine. The room was hot, but there was a chill growing in her chest.

Suddenly, the door opened, and Aiden came in, pushing a metal cart that was covered with a blanket. He paused and looked over at her a sneer spread across his lips.

"Ah, you're awake. Good. I'm almost ready," he said, and pushed the cart into the room closing the door behind him. He made his way over to her, stopping in front of her, along with the cart.

"Who are you? Why are you doing this?"

"Oh, I never introduced myself. I apologize. My name is Aiden Grey, and I'm a dark blood." He bowed with a sweep of his hand and stood back up grinning at her. "As to why I'm doing this? Well, it's in my nature as a dark blood to torture, but you're special Snow. You're the ice child of prophecy. I'll become infamous if I'm the one to turn you into one of us."

She gasped. "Turn me?"

"That's right. I have been thinking about what exactly I should do with you now that I have you, and I decided that by turning you into a dark blood, I would gain the favor of my king. He might even promote me from a knight to a rook. I would be the youngest rook in our history and one day I'll kill the king to take my place at the throne. But I'm getting ahead of myself. First I have to turn you and prove to my king how silly this prophecy bullshit really is."

"What prophecy? What exactly is it?"

He smirked. "You wouldn't know, would you? Not after the Silence. No one really knows, only the older monsters, or the dark bloods." He clapped his hands, and pulled over a chair from the table, setting it across from Snow and sitting down. "You know what? I'm going to tell it to you. Then I'm going to torture you to death and drink your blood. You'll be a dark blood by tomorrow morning, and I'll hand you over to my king by the afternoon."

Snow paled at his words and struggled in her bonds.

"Enough of that. Listen, for I'll only tell the story once."

She stopped. The cold feeling in her chest grew.

"Good, now where should I begin? Ah, yes, it goes something like this. A seer wrote the Great Book, and within it, there was a passage that spoke of an ice child, and her protector. It said that a great king would rule for centuries through fear and pain. But one day the ice child would be born and her protector bound to her by blood. They would appear before this king and vanquish him in blood and ice. Then they would bring about a new era of peace between monsters and humans."

"Don't we already have peace?" Snow asked trying to keep him talking, but he was already standing up again. The cold feeling in her chest was becoming unbearable and spreading out to her fingertips.

"Not really. You're young and easily tricked by the faux peace fed to you in the schools. Why do you think only monsters go to our school? It's because the humans refuse to integrate with them. You can live on the same street as a human, and in their neighborhoods, but put human children in school with monsters, and all hell breaks loose. You could say we are responsible for that. The dark bloods I mean. We have been attacking both sides for a long time and keeping the tension building. Your grandmother may have managed to force peace once, but we all knew it was only temporary. As long as my king rules, he will ensure the peace is never absolute. But enough of that. I'd like to begin if you don't mind," he sneered and pulled the sheet off of the metal tray revealing some very scary looking devices. Snow knew what some of them were, but she had never seen most of them. There was a metal pole with a point at one end next to a small hammer, there was a cigar cutter, as well as metal pliers, but she didn't recognize anything else. The sight of them made her pale further, and the cold icy feeling spreading from her chest reached a painful level.

He picked up the metal pliers. "How about I begin with your toenails?"

He moved closer to her. Suddenly, the cold feeling that had been building within Snow burned and burst from her body. She screamed.

CAIT HEARD a scream in the distance and knew it was Snow's. It made her blood run cold. She pushed her paws into the dirt to go faster. *Hold on Snow! I'm coming,* she thought and pushed herself even harder.

# CHAPTER SIXTEEN

The pain subsided, and Snow opened her eyes.

"You bitch! What have you done to me?" he yelled.

Aiden was a frozen statue all the way up to his neck. Actually, Snow realized, a thick coat of ice covered the whole cabin. Her breath fogged in front of her like smoke. She looked down at her hands and tested her bonds. The rope shattered at her command, and she was free.

"Where do you think you're going? I'm not through with you yet!"

Snow backtracked and stood in front of the boy. She slapped him hard enough to draw blood. Then she turned to the metal cart and picked up a roll of cotton. The brunette shoved it into his mouth.

"You're lucky I don't use the hammer on your head!" she yelled out as she ran for the door. Opening it, she made her way to the front door, only for it to open before her hand reached it. Her heart quickened in hope. The door opened. Standing before her were two dark bloods. Each one was armed with both a sword and a gun at their side.

They were dressed all in black and sewn into the fabric of their shirts, over their hearts, was a badge with the black pawn chess piece. They advanced on her. She didn't have much energy after that burst from earlier, but that didn't stop her from struggling with everything she had. One of the men karate chopped her in the back of the neck, and she fell to the ground. He picked her up and threw her over his shoulder like a sack of potatoes. She felt so weak she could barely lift her arms. Wherever that burst of ice had come from, it had used up her reserves and left her limp as the men carried her to a black SUV. For the second time that night, her vision darkened, and she slipped into unconsciousness.

CAIT CAME to a halt in front of a cabin only to sense that Snow wasn't there. Once again, she was too late. She phased back and ran naked into the cabin. In a room at the back, she found a dark blood vampire boy spitting cotton out of his mouth. She turned on him.

"Where is she!" she growled.

"Fuck you!"

She grabbed his neck, squeezing, her nails biting into the soft skin of his neck hard enough to draw blood.

"I'll kill you."

He choked out, "Then you'll never get to her in time."

She sneered but let go. He coughed. It was only then that Cait realized why the boy hadn't defended himself. His body was encased in a thick ice as well as the rest of the room. She could see her breath clouding around her.

"Where?"

"Xavier has her," he muttered.

"What..." She felt like the breath had been knocked out of her. He had her? Again, she had failed. He was going to take her most precious person from her again. Her wolf answered her.

"The oath will be fulfilled," It growled.

Cait nodded her head in agreement and turned to leave.

"You're just going to leave me here?"

She ignored him and left the cabin. A howl broke in the distance. She hated to admit it, but she was going to need help this time. Cait took off to meet up with Remus's pack. She just hoped they would be willing to go to battle with her.

When Cait reached Remus and the wolves he had brought from his clan, she had phased back to her wolf form.

"Cait, what happened?" Gwen asked. In her wolf form, she was by far the smallest. Her cocoa colored fur, smooth and silky, glinted in the moonlight. Remus was next to her, his form massive and daunting. He was the largest wolf there, but only slightly larger than Cait. It was normal for alphas to be the largest wolves. His fur was a reddish brown with patches of white mixed in. He shifted, getting Cait's full attention.

"Where is Snow?" he asked.

"The dark bloods have her," Cait growled baring her teeth.

The other wolves shifted uncomfortably. Remus barked, and they settled.

"I take it you need our help?" he asked.

Cait had suspected he would try to rub the fact that she

had failed in her face but his voice was even, and the question, was asked simply. She nodded.

"Will you go with me?"

"You mean will I battle alongside that last Fallon? To save your mate?" he asked. His voice staying level and calm.

"That is what I ask of you, yes."

His brown eyes glinted in what Cait was able to see as excitement before he raised his muzzle to the air and let loose a howl. The rest of his clan joined him in chorus. They sang.

"Two clans unite tonight. Fallon and Lander. To honor and to blood. Let our jaws crush, and our claws slice. Victory will be ours!"

Their howls quieted, and Remus met Cait's gaze. "I would be honored to kill some dark bloods alongside you. Lead the way. My teeth shall be your weapon and my body your shield. We fight for Lander! We fight for Fallon!"

Cait nodded. She felt the power flowing into her as Remus's wolf relinquished some of his command to her. With a bark from Cait, they were running, following her into battle, following her to Snow.

SNOW WOKE WITH A SORE NECK. She sat up rubbing it and looked around.

"The ice child awakens," a dark and insidious voice said from her left. She looked over to see a man who looked to be in his forties sitting on a throne. His hair was dark brown and pulled back into a ponytail at the base of his neck. He had a five o'clock shadow, and when she met his gaze, it was to meet blood red eyes. Snow gasped and tried to stand, but her body felt heavy and sluggish.

"Who are you? Where am I?" she whispered.

He smiled and waved his hand in a grand gesture of introduction. "My name? Why I'm sure, you know my name by now? But I shall welcome you to this Xavier's home. This is one of my many homes. Don't worry we are deep into the forest and deep into this castle. No one will bother us tonight. Well, except for your protector."

"Cait!" Snow yelled and attempted to stand once more only for her legs to feel like jello and give out. She plopped back onto the floor.

"Calm yourself, child. You are weak after awakening," he said as he stood from the throne.

"Awakening?"

"Yes! It truly is splendid. I wish I could have seen it in person, but my men took pictures, and what a sight!"

"What are you talking about?"

He walked towards her. With every step he took, she attempted to scoot back, but she was still weak, and his strides were strong and fast.

"The ice my dear. All the coldness your body can produce. It was truly beautiful." He reached her and crouched down beside her. Reaching out his hand, he took a strand of hair between his fingers. She jerked away from him, but he grabbed her face and forced her to meet his bloody gaze.

"And it will be mine."

She slapped his hand away. "No!"

Xavier chuckled and stood making his way back to the throne. "Say what you will. Tonight, the prophecy will be broken."

"How?"

He laughed darkly. "You didn't really think you and that

puny werewolf could really kill me, did you? You truly are a fool. I can't die."

"What do you mean?"

He sat down and faced her. "Well, I can die, but the likelihood of that wolf killing me are slim to none. I made sure of that when she was born."

"I don't understand."

He chuckled. "A child born without heart," he answered lazily.

Snow gasped. "You...you're the one that took her soul!"

"Yes! And how easy it was."

"How?"

He grinned and reached into his shirt pulling out a chain with a blue stone on the end. The stone glittered in the light. It was a sapphire. "With this."

Snow frowned. "A rock."

"It's a sapphire, and it was enchanted by a witch."

"Why?"

"To hold the soul of prophecy. Or at least one-half of it."

Snow gasped again and gazed at the stone. She could feel something inside of her being pulled towards it. "Give it to me," she said before she realized what she was saying.

Xavier laughed and tucked the stone back under his shirt. "I don't think so. It has served me well all these years giving me all the power I could ever want."

Snow felt the hot flush of anger. "It's not yours!"

Xavier stood again and looked across the throne room to the huge doors. Snow could hear a howling in the distance. Cait had come.

REMUS CHARGED at the metal gate separating the werewolves from the castle. The metal screamed and groaned as it bent then broke under his power. The werewolves charged through the courtyard. Several dark bloods appeared, pulling their swords and guns out, only to have their arms ripped off in a matter of seconds. Remus and Cait continued into the courtyard and burst through the door leading to the main hall. Cait's instincts were leading her to Snow. Remus followed her. He knew his wolves could handle a few dark bloods. The vampires were only as strong as their weapons. When his clan fought together, they were unstoppable. The hallways were cramped, and he had to let Cait go in front, but they stayed in their wolf forms.

The hallway opened up into a giant room, and Cait stopped. Remus came up beside her. In front of them were two large doors, but the reason Cait had stopped, was because of the boy standing in front of her. Remus recognized the boy from school, but he couldn't for the life of him remember the kid's name.

"Move!" Cait growled.

Aiden sneered, "Make me."

Remus stepped forward. The boy may be a student, but he was in their way. "I'll take care of him. You go on ahead," he spoke to Cait over their link. She nodded. Remus charged at the boy. Aiden jumped away from his place in front of the door to miss being eaten alive, and Remus followed him, chasing him. Cait took her chance and charged through the double doors. Her body slammed into them, breaking the wood from the force, and pushing them open. She skidded to a halt in what looked to be a throne room if the throne on the other end was any clue. She took in the room in front of her, her eyes first rested on Snow who was sitting on the ground. Her heart leaped with joy. Until her eyes were drawn away by a loud clapping.

"And the protector makes her appearance! Good to see you again, Cait. Did you miss me?"

"Xavier!" Cait snarled.

"The one and only."

"I'll kill you!"

He tsked, "I don't think so."

Cait growled and charged at him. Snow screamed as Cait crashed into the throne when Xavier jumped out of the way, flipped, and landed behind her. He pulled a sword from his side and held it out. Cait could smell the silver in the blade and only hesitated a second before charging again. Xavier jeered as she came within reach and he slashed at her shoulder. She whimpered in agony but knocked him to the ground. Her shoulder burned. The wound wouldn't heal right away like usual, but she had fought many an opponent in the past, who thought they could get one over on her by using silver. She wasn't going to go down easy!

Cait circled the man that had made her life a living hell. She couldn't wait to feel his bones crunch between her jaws.

"You can't kill me Cait," he taunted.

"Watch me!" She lunged, but he rolled out of the way. They circled each other again.

"You are too weak. A child without heart can't kill me!"

Cait growled and made to lunge at him again, but he pulled a necklace out from under his shirt, and Cait suddenly felt weak. What was that?

"This is your heart Cait!"

"What?"

"Yes, I've had it all along. I've had your soul since the day you were born, and the seer told me you would be the protector."

Cait was at a loss for words. She could feel the pull to the stone and knew what he was saying was the truth.

"It's amazing. The things the Sluagh, the monsters in the shadows, will do for the right price. I asked for your soul, and they delivered by stealing it from you while you slept in your mother's arms. I have the power of the protector. You can't defeat me."

Cait snarled, charged at the man, and slashed her claws at him. He managed to prevent her from getting the necklace, but her nails bit into his back electing a scream from him. He stumbled back.

"You bitch!" he yelled.

Cait felt her anger rising. Xavier began to laugh. The werewolf watched as the wound instantly closed, leaving only blood, and ripped clothing behind. "I told you I couldn't die."

The werewolf felt a sinking feeling in her gut and jumped at Xavier attempting to sink her teeth into him. His long sword came up and connected with the side of her neck. It burned, but she pushed through it enough to sink her teeth into his shoulder. He cried out, but she held on biting down harder. Xavier screamed and raised his sword.

"Cait!" Snow screamed.

The sword pierced her shoulder, and she bit down harder as the blade burned its way inside of her. She shook her head, tearing the skin beneath her teeth, and ripping a chunk of his shoulder off as she jumped back. Xavier groaned as he staggered. His blade was sticking out of Cait's shoulder as she stumbled back, and fell to the ground, spitting out the chunk of flesh she had taken with her.

Xavier fell to the floor and inspected his shoulder. His mind was numb with pain as he watched the bone and skin reproduce and stitch back together. Cait could feel the silver from the sword as it began to enter her bloodstream like poison. Her power was waning, and her body was beginning to feel heavier, as she struggled to stand.

"Cait!" Snow pushed herself up but struggled to keep her balance. She still felt weak, but she had to get to the werewolf.

Deep laughter filled the air and Snow looked at the dark blood. He was standing again across from Cait. "Is that all the great protector has?" he taunted.

Cait snarled and pushed herself back up.

"Come on!" he yelled. "Or do I need to move on to the ice child?"

The werewolf growled and charged. Snow felt dread in her stomach as she saw a glint of silver. Xavier was hiding a dagger behind his back. He was going to kill her. He was going to kill Cait. He was going to kill her mate. Snow felt the burn of ice burst from her chest and out her fingertips again. She could feel the power flowing out of her and watched as ice spread from her as if she was winter itself.

The floor beneath her instantly froze and traveled with speed towards Xavier. He didn't even have the chance to scream as his body was encased in ice all the way up to his shoulders, and Cait's jaws clamped over his head, tearing it from his neck. The werewolf landed covered in blood and spit out the head of the man who had cost her so much in her life. She fell to the ground.

"Cait!" Snow stumbled and skidded across the ice until

she was standing next to the werewolf. The redhead transformed back into the woman as the wolf's words rang out in her mind.

'The oath has been fulfilled, the promise kept, the betrayal is forgiven. We are one once more.'

"Hey, stay awake," Snow whispered as she rolled Cait over so she could touch her face. The redhead groaned from the movement.

"Take out the sword," she moaned in pain.

Snow hesitated, but rested the werewolf's head in her lap, and wrapped both of her hands around the hilt of the long sword. She gripped and pulled. It was released with a sickening slurping sound and blood began to flow freely from the wound it made. Snow cried out and held her hands over the wound to slow down the bleeding.

"Cait!"

"It's fine...it will...heal," she gasped out.

"There's too much blood!"

"The...necklace." Cait lifted her shaky hand and pointed to where she had spat out Xavier's head. Snow grimaced but gently set Cait down and ran over to it. She picked up the bloody stone, pulling it off the severed neck, and felt her stomach roll. She ran back over to Cait and kneeled down beside her.

"What do I do?" she asked.

"I...don't...know."

"You big dummy! What do you mean you don't know? Cait!"

"Kiss me," she whispered out.

"What?"

"Accept my devotion."

"What are you talking about now?"

"You promised you would think about it."

Snow remembered their first kiss and blushed. Gwen had told her the kiss was to tell Cait, as well as the wolf, that she would think about accepting the imprint. Now it seemed that Cait wanted an answer. Did she want to be her friend or her lover? What sort of bond would they create? Snow felt her heart-rate pick up, thumping in her chest. Cait coughed up blood. Snow helped her sit up a little bit. This woman was completely devoted to her. She had never wavered from her loyalty. She had given everything for her.

Snow smiled. The answer really was a simple one. She tilted Cait's head back, one hand on her chin, and touched her cold lips to bloody ones. Cait gasped at the feeling of the girl's cold but soft lips. She felt Snow's hand touch her chest while the other held her head up. Suddenly, there was a warm burning feeling on her chest where Snow's hand was. She groaned but the pain increased. Snow pulled back when the woman beneath her whimpered to see the werewolf grimacing.

"Cait?"

"It's hot," she moaned out, and Snow looked down to see that the sapphire had broken into pieces. She gasped.

"What?"

"I feel so hot." Cait breathed. Snow placed her hand against the woman's head, but she felt normal to her. Cait grabbed Snow's hand and placed it over her heart again. She let out a breath.

"What is that heaviness that I feel?" Cait whispered.

As Snow's hand was placed over the werewolf's heart, she felt her own calling out to it. She felt her chest fill with the warmth that was traveling up from her hand and into her heart. She gasped as she felt something connect inside of her as if she was filled with another presence. A feeling of wholeness settled over her.

“Do you feel that?” Snow asked.

“I feel—”

“What Cait? What do you feel?”

“I feel complete.”

CHAPTER

# SEVENTEEN

When Cait woke, it was to an immense feeling of comfort, and warmth. She made to sit up only to feel a weight against her side. Looking down she saw Snow sleeping next to her. The girl had her arm slung over Cait's waist and her head buried into the pillow. The werewolf smiled and trailed her fingertips along the girl's arm. The brunette broke out in goosebumps and rubbed her eyes as she woke. Snow yawned.

"Hey," Cait whispered.

"Morning--" Snow's eyes shot open. "Cait!" She pulled the woman into her arms fully.

Cait chuckled. "Hey, calm down."

Snow buried her face into the werewolf's neck, and Cait was shocked to hear sniffles. "Hey, what's the matter."

Snow pulled back to meet her gaze. "I didn't think you would ever wake up."

The redhead frowned. "How long was I out for?"

"Four days."

Cait sighed. "It's because of the silver. It usually takes longer for me to heal from those wounds."

Snow nodded. “You just fully healed yesterday and Gwen said you would be waking up soon.”

Cait smiled and took a strand of white hair between her fingers. “Your hair...”

Snow smiled. “Yeah. Gwen thinks it’s from my powers awakening fully.”

The werewolf smiled and tucked the strand behind the girl’s ear. “You accepted.”

Snow blushed and nodded.

“You were sure.” It was a statement but the girl answered anyway.

“I am.”

Cait smiled and bent down to kiss her. It was tender and light. The werewolf pulled back. “Thank you.”

Snow smiled but seemed to hesitate before speaking. “I want to go through the blood bond of lovers with you.”

Cait paused in playing with her hair and met her gaze. “Are you ready? We just--”

She cut her off. “I’ve never been more ready for anything in my life. I want to be yours and for you to be mine, fully.”

The werewolf smiled, and their lips touched once more but with more force this time. Cait ran her fingers through Snow’s hair, and tilted the girl's chin, before trailing her hand down the slender neck to rest above her heart. She could feel it beating faster, and their tongues danced against each other. She pulled back when she felt something inside her own chest warm up.

“Whoa.”

“What?” Snow asked.

Cait studied her hand that was resting against Snow’s chest. It felt hot underneath. She felt like her own heart was calling out to the beating of Snow's. "Nothing, it just felt funny."

Snow smiled. "It should."

The werewolf looked up at her questioningly.

Snow giggled. "It will never be said again that you are a werewolf without heart. It calls to mine and mine answers back."

The redhead felt the sting of tears at the girl's softly spoken words.

"YOU GUYS ARE SURE ABOUT THIS?" Gwen asked as she followed Cait and Snow into Cait's apartment.

"For the last time Gwen, we are sure."

Cait looked thoughtfully at her living room. It had been cleared of the usual things, and all that remained was her king sized bed. "Will you be in the next room or in here Gwen?"

The omega sighed and rested against the wall. "It's really up to you. Do you get performance anxiety?"

Cait growled.

"I'm serious. Some people do. I can be in the other room to make it easier. Just having me in the vicinity should keep your wolf in check. When it comes out during the ritual, it will sense me nearby, and that will calm it down. So I can be in the room with you, or I can be in the kitchen. Either is fine."

Snow cleared her throat. "Um, I prefer the kitchen."

Gwen chuckled and pushed off the wall. "The kitchen it is then. Now, do you two remember everything we talked about?"

They both nodded.

"Well, have at it then!" She giggled when Snow blushed, gave a mock salute, and walked over to the next room, pulling out a book from her bag.

The girl didn't know how to feel about the omega reading a book while they did the deed in the next room but she guessed it was necessary. She sighed and looked up when she felt Cait pulling her towards the bed.

"Come."

Snow nodded and let the werewolf guide her. She settled at the head of the bed and lay there as Cait kneeled between her legs. Snow was wearing a yellow summer dress, and Cait trailed her hands up the girl's legs, drawing the dress along with it. She paused when she reached mid thigh. She could feel how tense Snow was.

"Relax," she whispered as she leaned down and gently kissed the girl. It was slow and light at first, but Snow responded quickly and moved to deepen the kiss by slipping her tongue into the werewolf's warm depths. Cait moaned and began drawing circles on Snow's thighs.

Snow could feel herself heating up as the werewolf swirled her tongue in her mouth dominating every part she touched. She moaned and pushed up to meet Cait's chest. Suddenly, the woman pulled back causing Snow to groan in annoyance.

"Just a minute." The werewolf chuckled as she pulled off her button up and slowly slipped Snow's dress over her head throwing it to the floor. Their bras came next leaving only their underwear. Cait hovered over the girl taking in every inch of her.

"Beautiful," she breathed. The brunette blushed and moved to cover herself, but Cait stopped her.

"Don't. I want to see you," she whispered. She raised her hand up to circle the girl's left nipple. It beaded up at the attention and Cait bent down to capture it in her mouth. Snow groaned and buried her hands in the woman's hair.

"Cait," Snow breathed as she felt teeth tease her breast. When the woman bit gently, electricity shot straight to the girl's sex. It throbbed for attention.

The redhead settled fully between Snow's legs groaning at the feeling of the girl's hot center touching her abs.

"Oh, Snow," she moaned and trailed hot kisses up from the breast to settle on her neck.

The brunette moaned and began grinding. The werewolf could feel her getting wet. She grabbed the girl's ass and pushed into her, hard. Snow gasped.

"God."

"Cait, will do." The werewolf chuckled and captured the neglected nipple giving it the attention it demanded.

"Shut up," Snow breathed.

Cait bit down eliciting a moan from the girl beneath her. "Be nice."

Snow groaned as she ground harder into the woman and dug her nails slightly into her back.

"Cait!" she whined.

The werewolf could feel how soaked the girl was and could feel her throbbing through her underwear. She moaned as she trailed hot kisses down Snow's stomach, stopping to dip her tongue into her belly button, making her gasp. She continued until she reached her destination, and hooked her fingers under the band of the girl's panties, pulling it down. Snow lifted her hips to let the werewolf undress her and watched as the last barrier was tossed over the side of the bed. The brunette was looking at her through hooded eyes and noticed when the werewolf's flashed gold. Cait nudged her way between pale thighs, hovering over her mate carefully. Her pupils dilated from the smell of arousal.

Cait groaned. "Snow." Then her tongue slipped between silken folds.

Snow gasped. Her hands going straight for the werewolf's tresses and burying her fingers into them. She watched the werewolf raptly. All of her attention was drawn to the eyes that were flickering between gold and electric blue. She knew the redhead was changing, merging, both the wolf and woman were one. Cait trailed her tongue along the soft flesh, stopping at the little nub at the top. She sucked it in between her teeth then circled it with her tongue. She heard a low groan.

"More."

Cait hummed and bit down gently on the hard nub. Snow moaned, jerked, tightening her thighs around the werewolf's head, as tingles of pleasure began to build in the form of heat at her center. It throbbed, and she found herself wanting something more, but she wasn't sure what exactly. She wanted to be closer to the werewolf, whole, one.

"Please!" Snow breathed and began to grind harder into Cait.

The werewolf sucked once more on the hard nub and could feel the girl was wet and ready. She brought her hand up and gently parted Snow's moist folds, dipping a single finger inside her mate. The girl gasped, arms clutching Cait's shoulders tightly. Her mouth opened slightly.

The werewolf slowly thrust forward, watching her finger slowly disappear inside the silky depths. About halfway through she felt a thin layer of flesh block her. Snow gasped. Cait paused the implications of what it meant hit her, making her heart swell with love. She drew herself up and met Snow's lips again, pouring her gratitude, and love into the kiss.

The girl moaned, hips undulating with want. The feel of Cait inside of her was wonderful.

"Cait."

The werewolf nodded, her body trembling with want and the need to mate growing stronger. Mine! She felt her teeth lengthen and with a forceful push, she broke Snow's hymen, filling the girl to the hilt. The girl cried out and tensed, the combination of pain, and sweet pleasure mixing.

Cait deepened the kiss, splitting her attention, allowing the pleasure to begin to dominate the pain. Cait paused allowing Snow to settle into the discomfort and begin to relax again.

"I got you," she whispered against the girl's lips.

Snow nodded and broke the kiss."It's okay."

Cait smiled and began to move, slowly thrusting in and out. She groaned as Snow's velvety walls constricted around her fingers, the wetness coating her hand. Snow whimpered from the pleasure assaulting her in waves. She moved her hips in time with her lovers, sending Cait deeper within. Soon the werewolf picked up her pace adding a third finger. Snow clutched at the red head groaning in pleasure. She dug her nails into Cait's back, raking them down desperately, as the werewolf slammed into her again and again.

Together they moved their bodies a blur of movement, and pleasure. They thrust together wildly. Snow could feel her peak building. She whispered Cait's name, again and again, slamming her hips up to meet the wet fingers that slipped easily into her over and over again. Cait felt Snow's walls flutter around her fingers, her own sex tightening in sympathy.

She thrust once, twice, and on the third Snow screamed and came undone in her arms screaming her name.

Cait felt the werewolf slam against her mental cage and burst forth. Mine! Cait burst into her wolf form. She was suddenly hovering over Snow on all fours. Snow was weak from her orgasm, but she could remember what Gwen had told her to do. She picked herself up, so she was laying back on her elbows and bared her throat in submission.

"I am yours, from the break of dawn to the descent of night, from now until the end of eternity." She gasped out and tensed as the teeth descended on her shoulder and bit down. Snow screamed in pain, but the teeth were gone as soon as they had been there. She dropped from her elbows to the bed. The feeling of a tongue trailing along the bite settled her and eased the pain.

"It's a knot."

"Hmm?"

Cait smiled at the girl beneath her who had been so brave only a second ago.

"The bite heals in the form of a Celtic knot. I had always wondered how my mother got the mark. I always just thought it was a tattoo, but she told me it was the Fallon Clan's symbol."

"What does it look like?" Snow asked.

"It's the Quaternary knot."

"Mmm?" Snow hummed and moved to try and look at it, making Cait chuckle.

"It's the four-cornered Celtic knot, so it's kind of hard to explain what it looks like, but I know what it means. My mother told me."

"What?" Snow asked meeting her gaze.

"It's a symbol of protection. I will always protect you, Snow."

Snow smiled at the finality of everything and spoke meeting the gaze of soft blue eyes. She whispered, "I love you Cait."

The werewolf smiled. "And I, you. I am yours for eternity. You are my heart."

A tear trailed down Snow's cheek, and Cait leaned in to capture it with her tongue. The two lay in each other's arms as they fell asleep.

# EPILOGUE

Snow was nervous. Cait could feel the anxiety coming off her in waves.

"Everything will be fine."

She turned to the werewolf. "Are you sure I should be here? It's supposed to be special."

Cait chuckled. "It's fine. You're my mate. You go where I go even to the moon festival."

"But--" Snow was cut off when a voice called out to them. Gwen met them at the door.

"Hey, you're finally here! The moon is almost at its peak." She grabbed Snow's hand and dragged her through the house and out into the backyard.

All the werewolves of the Lander clan had transformed and were seated, scattered across the lawn, staring up at the sky. Gwen pulled Snow to a soft patch of grass and sat them down. "You don't want to miss this. Don't worry; I'll be your interpreter." The omega smiled and faced the sky.

Snow looked up in time to see golden eyes watching her. Her white wolf had joined the ranks and turned to face the sky as well. A moment of silence passed, and she heard Gwen mutter beside her, "They are going to begin, now!"

Suddenly, a large russet wolf with white patches rose his muzzle and let out a booming howl. He was by far the largest one there.

Gwen leaned over to her and whispered, "That's Remus."

Snow nodded and listened to his howl as Gwen interpreted.

He sang, "I sing a song to the great full moon. Let all who hear it answer. Another cycle has completed. I sing a song with my clan. The strong Lander's. I sing a song with a friend, the great protector, Fallon. Let the moon hear our chorus, let our friends answer our call, our journey is long and hard, but our clan is strong. Sing Lander, sing Fallon."

All the wolves lifted their heads and sang in chorus as one mighty sound. It sent a shiver down Snow's spine from the sheer power behind the howls. The wolves slowly began to taper off until only one wolf was howling. It was Cait.

The white wolf drew in a breath and sang, "I sing a song to the great full moon. Let all who hear it answer. I stand among the honorable Lander's as the lone Fallon. I sing a song of my devotion. I, the surviving Fallon, sing to my clansmen from up above. Snow Bennett is your new sister. She is my mate and my love. I sing an oath to her. Hear this oath. I, Cait Fallon, shall live on and continue the Fallon legacy. The Fallon's will be strong once more. I am no longer the child without heart, and I devote all of it to my mate. We will be strong. We will live long. We will be blood bound."

The wolves lifted and answered her song in chorus. Each singing with their own unique voice. As Gwen translated Cait's song, Snow felt tears trailing down her cheeks. She was the happiest she had ever been. For so long, she had felt lost and alone. Now, she had a family and a lover. She was part of something bigger. She was in love, and she was whole.

## Author's note

Dear Reader,

I want to personally thank you for taking the time to read this story. This book has been sitting in a closet gathering dust for years, and it wasn't until a good friend asked about it over dinner and demanded that I publish it, that I decided to pull it out and fix it up. This story has always been near and dear to my heart as I wrote it after a really bad break-up. At that time this story gave me great joy and helped me pull through a dark time.

I hope you, Reader, have found some joy in reading it and I hope it made your heart flutter at moments. I know it did for mine when I dusted it off and read through it after all these years.

Thank you,

Idella Breen

Happy reading!

loved Cait's songs. Sniff. Tears running down her cheeks. She was the happiest she had ever been. For so long she had Gilbert and alone. Now she had a family and a [illegible]. She was part of something bigger, she was in love, and that [illegible]

*

## Author's Note

[illegible]

# AUTHOR'S NOTE

Hi! I hope you enjoyed this book. I had a lot of fun writing it. If you're interested in keeping up with the latest published books in this series and others, consider joining my email list.

Get your free ebook! By joining my reader's group you can get Soul Awakened, book 2 of Fire & Ice, for free.

Click Here!

Happy reading,

Idella Breen


facebook.com/Idella-Breen-573566509481476

x.com/IdellaBreen

instagram.com/idellabreen

amazon.com/Idella-Breen/e/B01I93Z9DM/ref=sr_ntt_srch_lnk_2?qid=1538940237&sr=8-2

# ALSO BY IDELLA BREEN

<u>The Dance of The Firefly</u>

When The Clock Strikes Nothing

<u>Fire& Ice:</u>

Blood Bound

Soul Awakened

Lover Eternal/Adventures of Elena the Werewolf

Pack Mentality

The King of Brimstone and Bones

<u>Blood & Ember:</u>

Blood Eternal: Book One of Salt

<u>Witch Twin Chronicles:</u>

Unrestricted Magic

<u>Eternal Soul Trilogy:</u>

Bone Walker

<u>Water & Bone:</u>

The Girl Who Leapt Worlds

<u>Novellas:</u>

Feeders and Bleeders

Descent

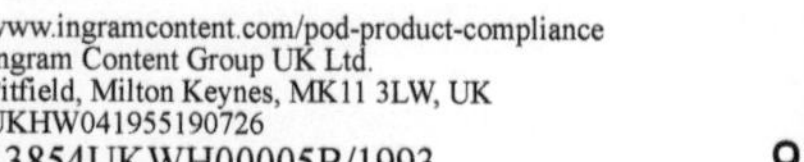
www.ingramcontent.com/pod-product-compliance
Ingram Content Group UK Ltd.
Pitfield, Milton Keynes, MK11 3LW, UK
UKHW041955190726
13854UKWH00005B/1993

9 798215 031230